Tea and Mystery

The three sat in the kitchen, around a spacious, clean-lined oak table, while George lit a burner under a kettle on an enormous, industrial-looking stove. Outside, through huge sliding-glass doors that opened on to a riverside terrace, they could see the rain whipping down in sheets. Dewey talked about the changes in the library until the tea was ready.

"All right, now, you two. I sense that there is something up here," Captain Booker said, accepting a cup of tea from George.

"Bookie," Dewey said, "before you tell me I'm loony, I think you should hear me out."

"Yes, Dewey?"

"Bookie, have you looked carefully into how Donald Irish died?"

The question obviously surprised him. "I'm not sure just what you mean, Dewey. Charlie O'Donovan examined him, you know. The coroner was satisfied—"

"Bookie, I think Donald Irish was murdered."

"What put you on to this idea, Dewey?" he asked.

"The horse."

A Dewey James Mystery

A Slay at the Races

Kate Morgan

B
BERKLEY BOOKS, NEW YORK

A SLAY AT THE RACES

A Berkley Book / published by arrangement with
the author

PRINTING HISTORY
Berkley edition / October 1990

ISBN: 0-425-12166-6

PRINTED IN THE UNITED STATES OF AMERICA

10 9 8 7 6 5 4 3 2 1

To my mother,
who loves a good murder;
and my father,
who remains within the law

1

DEWEY JAMES HEARD a heavy tread behind her and felt hot, damp breath on her neck. Involuntarily she jumped, dropping the grocery bag she carried. Its contents spilled out as Dewey spun around.

"Starbuck!" she said reprovingly. "You gave me a fright." A tall, athletically built woman with short silver hair, she looked straight into the eyes of an old chestnut mare and laughed as the horse nuzzled her. "How did you get out of your stall? Back you go, you silly horse."

With an expertise that spoke of long experience, Dewey James took hold of the mare and led her around the side of the small stable to her box. It was an early evening toward the end of May, and the sun had just begun to turn the surrounding countryside a pale red-gold. Dewey noted and approved the sunset as she led the mare along. "I must be getting forgetful, Starbuck," she muttered. "Leaving your stall door open. You silly thing. What if you had wandered off somewhere?"

They reached the small building, newly painted a bright red but otherwise sadly in need of repair. There were two stalls inside, but Starbuck dwelt here in solitary splendor. "Well, now we'll see about closing the barn door after the horse is back!" said Dewey to herself.

She gave the mare a kindly shove. "Stand not upon the order of your going," she muttered and swung the box door shut. She slipped a worn wooden bar through its brackets to hold the door in place. Then she rummaged for a minute in a well-worn handbag and, after a brief search, came up with a small, rather weather-beaten carrot. "Only because I love you," she told the horse. "You're the reason, you know, that everyone thinks I'm losing my grip. But it would be unthinkable not to have a carrot for you when you need it." The mare munched noisily as Dewey prattled. "It is not old age, however. I'm not some old lady who carries *food* around. No matter what they think."

Indeed, there was truth in what Dewey James said. The people of her hometown of Hamilton did think she was mildly lunatic—but this was not news. They had thought so for most of her sixty-odd years. Some of them waited with a knowing forbearance for the day when Dewey dropped the ball completely.

But Dewey persisted. She clung steadfast to an eccentric code all her own, appearing oblivious to the smiles and winks of her neighbors. In her thirty years as the town librarian, she established herself as a character. Some Hamiltonians assumed that Dewey had slipped, long ago, into an obscure literary dementia, for she peppered her speech with quotations from dead-and-gone authors—Shakespeare, Browning, Gilbert and Sullivan, Catullus. (Some of her sources did not even speak English!) And she was iconoclastic, welcoming exuberant teenagers to the reference room. "It encourages them to spend time here," she'd say, when people complained about noise. And, of course, she was right. Dewey was often right: an annoying trait. No wonder people said she was a little—well, you know.

Not to mention the fact that she talked to her horse. Dewey gave Starbuck's nose a final loving pat and set off across the small corner of pasture that separated the little stable from her large, rambling frame house. George Farnham was coming at teatime—which, in George's case, really meant for a drink—and Dewey still had to change. She glanced at her watch.

"I do hope he's late," she said under her breath, stopping to pick up the groceries where they had fallen. She gazed sadly at dozens of little red berries, which had spilled out of their box and nestled in various corners and niches in the gravel driveway. "Why on earth did I buy lingonberries?"

The raccoons, at least, would have a field day, thought

Dewey, as she marched up the driveway, groceries piled perilously in her arms, and let herself in at the kitchen door.

With the groceries stashed, Dewey bathed and changed and was ready when Isaiah, a large and friendly labrador retriever, announced George Farnham's arrival with a series of welcoming barks. Dewey opened the screen door to the front porch.

"Hello, Dewey," George said warmly, planting a friendly kiss on her cheek. He held out a bunch of wild geraniums. "For you, my dear." He was a sturdily built man of about Dewey's age, graying but still good-looking, with an enormous fund of energy. He was devoted to Dewey.

"Thank you, George. Come in, come in. Down, Isaiah," she told the dog, who had risen to plant his enormous front paws on George's chest.

Dewey and George had been friends for half a century. As a child, Dewey had been fiercely excluded from George's "Girl-haters Club." But as adults they had long been allies. Farnham was a prosperous lawyer—although now he practiced only part-time—and he had served for two decades as town council president. In this capacity, he had long enjoyed supporting Dewey in her more outrageous schemes, especially when they raised staid eyebrows in Hamilton.

Dewey in turn owed him a great deal, for he had come to her rescue more than once in a controversy of her own making. In 1970, when she'd hung an enormous peace symbol in the library, she had nearly lost her job. Even her husband Brendan, who was Hamilton's chief of police, had not supported her. But George had spoken out and turned the tide.

Both Dewey and George had been widowed for several years, and in recent months George had begun to show alarming signs of wishing to press his suit. This turn of events flustered Dewey. She was now steering a perilously polite course, attempting on the one hand to maintain her friendship, and on the other to discourage George's amorous proclivities. The job was difficult. Life was so much simpler when you could just be chums. Really.

Now Dewey put George's wild geraniums in a vase and the two moved into the parlor, with Isaiah tailing hopefully along behind. There would be drinks, possibly hors d'oeuvres. Perhaps some cheese, for a faithful dog.

"You're looking well, Dewey. Your trip to California seems to have agreed with you."

"Grace is so happy in San Diego, George. It was good for the spirit to see her so cheerful. I can't imagine liking California myself—too much sunshine. But she loves it. And she seems to have quite a nice young man, too."

"Oh? Anything serious?"

"George, I'm her mother. For all I'm aged and poor and slow. I should be the last to know if it were serious." She handed him a stiff gin and tonic.

"Thanks, my dear." George accepted the drink. "Dewey, do I detect a tinge of self-pity in your usually reasoned thinking?"

"No, don't be silly, George. Although at times like this I do miss Brendan. He was always in Grace's confidence, you know. She told him absolutely everything. And he told *me* just a little of it. So I felt more . . . in the picture."

"I imagine that when you've got the chief of detectives for a father, you might just as well be up front. Save him a lot of guesswork at dinnertime."

Dewey laughed. Her husband, Brendan James, had been the head of Hamilton's tiny police force for thirty years. But his duties in their quiet little town had rarely included detective work.

From a table near the bar Dewey produced a small plate—chipped, but unmistakably Crown Derby. It held some rather soggy crackers, accompanied by a dubious-looking dip. George glanced involuntarily at Isaiah as he accepted a cracker from the proffered plate.

"Don't you give my hors d'oeuvres to the dog, George. You really are a food snob."

Dewey never misses a trick, thought George. "I'm not a snob," he protested, popping the soggy cracker in his mouth. "Isaiah looks hungry."

"He always looks hungry. That's just the way he looks; it's his *metier*. Now, tell me what the news is."

"Did I say there was news?"

"No, but there is. You can't even fool me some of the time."

"Well, it's not really that exciting. But I thought you'd like to know. Guess who'll be riding for Barnhouse Stables in the point-to-point?"

Every year, the citizens of Hamilton turned out in large numbers for this horse race—an informal cross-country meet in which all were welcome to participate. By national racing standards, the Hamilton Cup was a non-event; it was really more like a town fair, and always made for momentous festivity. Everyone turned out to picnic on cold chicken and deviled eggs, lemonade and Bloody Marys.

"Don't make me guess, George." Dewey bit into a cracker and looked apologetically at her friend. "These are soggy, George. Sorry." She handed the cracker to Isaiah. "Which horse, do you mean? Let me see if I can guess. Midnight Blue."

"Right you are. But—this is the interesting part. Leslie is putting up a new jockey."

"You're joking!"

Dewey's neighbor, Leslie Downing, owned a small but very fine racing stable, which had become rather prosperous over the years. Naturally, she used a variety of professional jockeys for the many international races that she entered. But it was a standing joke in Hamilton that she always allowed her manager, Hugh Shields, to ride the annual Hamilton point-to-point. And although there were several good stables in the area, all with sturdy entrants and better-than-average jockeys, it always seemed that Hugh Shields somehow won the day.

This little equestrian miracle had been played out so many times that it was impossible to think of another course of events. The whole tradition was rather like a little latter-day passion play; and the hero was good old Hugh Shields.

"Not a joke, I promise. Everyone is buzzing about it."

"Oh, dear. Is Hugh hurt?"

"I saw him this morning lifting a fifty-pound sack of oats. He's fit as a fiddle."

"Well, maybe there's a real purse this year."

"No purse. Proceeds to the Hornets, as always." The Hamilton Hornets were the local high-school basketball team, and the town's pride and joy.

"Has Hugh fallen out of favor, then?"

"Must have. I ran into Louella Smith this morning, and she'd just come from having her hair done, and even Doris doesn't know what's behind it."

"Ye gods, it doth amaze me."

Doris Bock, hairdresser to Hamilton's ladies for forty-five years, was usually the most reliable source for information of this kind.

"Nobody knows anything. He must be in the doghouse, though." George glanced at Isaiah, who threw him a baleful look. "No offense, pal." George slipped him a cracker. "I think that new beau of hers must be behind it. Donald whats-it, from the bank. Dewey, everyone is counting on you to find out."

"Donald Irish. George, I don't *know* Leslie Downing. Well, not well enough to ask her right out about something like this!"

"We're counting on you, Dewey." George was firm. "Use some of your subtle ways, m'dear, and find out what's behind it."

"Well, there is that currycomb of hers that I borrowed for Starbuck last month. I suppose I could return it." She smiled.

"That's right. Now, Dewey, let me take you to dinner." George reached over and took one of her hands in his. Dewey leaped up out of her chair.

"No, George, thank you—I have so much to do. Besides, where would we go?"

"Panella's," said George simply, standing and looking at her. "A bottle of Ruffino, a little candlelight . . ."

"Oh, George."

"Come on, Dewey." He assumed a comical, moonstruck expression and looked deep into her eyes. "Tortellini," he said, in his best Italian, "*a l'arabbiata, ma non tropo*. Osso bucco. Saltimbocca. Parmeggiana. Spumoni!"

Dewey laughed. "Well, I shouldn't. There is so much to do. But if you promise to get me home early, then I will."

George put on his most solemn face and placed a hand over his heart. Dewey laughed.

"Just let me get my sweater."

George smiled with gratification and began to clear away the glasses. "Come on, Isaiah old boy," he said, "we're on KP."

Dewey climbed the stairs to her bedroom and searched in the twilight for her favorite sweater—a thick, cotton cardigan of eye-popping purple that she wore for every imaginable occasion. As she put it on, she glanced in the dressing table mirror and let out a little sigh. "Same old face, every time I look," she said to no one. Just then, through the window, a movement caught her eye in the little field outside. Starbuck was munching on grass. A strange sense of disorientation shivered through Dewey as she moved closer to the window to look out. This was strange, very peculiar indeed. She might be a forgetful old lady, but she was *not* a lunatic. Dewey had been very careful about locking that door to Starbuck's box. Someone had opened it.

"George!" cried Dewey, charging down the stairs. "George, they're after Starbuck!"

It took some time to get the old mare back in her stall, and finally George succeeded in calming Dewey's fears. They set out for town, and by the time they reached Panella's, Dewey's apprehension had vanished. George pooh-poohed—but very sweetly—her assurances that she had locked Starbuck's stall door; and his skepticism buoyed her, dispelling her uneasiness.

George was full of kindly concern, but kept his ardor, such as it was, at a friendly, bantering level. Over dinner, he filled Dewey in on other Hamilton news. The other hot issue in town was a proposal from a real estate group to purchase a large group of farm properties, just north of town, for residential development. Some of the property belonged to the town, and all of it would need to be rezoned if the proposal was accepted. Predictably, the issue had aroused heated emotions. Some people stood to make a pot of money if the deal was to go through. They passed the evening in spirited discussion of the plan, and George brought her home early as promised. Dewey had a good night's sleep.

With the rising sun the next morning, however, some of Dewey's earlier uneasiness reappeared, and she decided that something had to be done about securing Starbuck's stall door. She wasn't particularly worried that there was real mischief afoot; the perpetrator was probably just one of the nearby kids having fun. But Dewey adored Starbuck and was inclined to worry about her. She hoped that nobody was trying to sneak off for a moonlight ride on the old mare. If Starbuck was to break a leg, Dewey would just as soon shoot herself as put her old friend down.

And if there were real prowlers in the neighborhood, she would hear of it at Barnhouse, for the Downing stables had a huge staff, and many people slept on the premises. It was only right, thought Dewey; those horses were extremely valuable.

Thus justified—at least in her own mind—she resolved to set out right after breakfast for Barnhouse, there to discover, if she could, the reason behind Leslie Downing's mysterious break with tradition.

2

AT FIFTY-TWO years of age, Leslie Downing was still considered the most beautiful woman in Hamilton. How much this opinion owed to her prominence in the town, it is difficult to say; for certainly what people take for beauty is often merely self-assurance, which lends grace to the most trivial of gestures. And of this grace, Leslie Downing was most decidedly possessed.

Her belief in her own convictions was deeply rooted, and it expressed itself in everything she did. People even noticed it in the shops and markets of the little town; while her neighbors weighed the merits of various on-sale brands, Leslie Downing never wavered. She took what she wanted and was on her way.

With such self-assurance, she was an excellent horsewoman. The sensitive and highly strung thoroughbreds in her stable responded easily to her calm directives, for horses, very much like people, enjoy being told what to do.

And so on the strength of this single-mindedness—with the aid, it is true, of a small personal fortune and large alimony payments from her former husband—Leslie Downing had built the racing stables at Barnhouse. She could size up a horse a mile away, and had never been suckered by even the most persuasive of horse traders. Her success was not surprising, and her fortunes appeared to improve all the time. Last year her filly Meretricious had placed (by a nose, in a photo finish) in the prestigious Hunterdon Stakes, the biggest race this side of the Derby.

Leslie Downing did not suffer fools gladly—human or

equine. Thus it was all the more interesting to the good watchers of Hamilton that she was lately rumored to be romantically involved with Donald Irish. Not that everyone in Hamilton counted him a fool; by no means. Divorced, like Leslie, Irish had recently arrived in Hamilton to take up the position of manager at the Warren State Savings and Loan. He was said to have a ready wit, an easy charm, and tremendous financial abilities. He had taken a strong interest in the financial future of Barnhouse, and now spent a great deal of time there.

Leslie Downing had few really close friends in Hamilton. In spite of her beauty and her wealth, she had never, in the twenty years since her divorce, been known to be in love. This romance, therefore, had given rise to interested speculation.

Dewey herself had wondered briefly about it, but she knew as well as anyone that "a single man in possession of a good fortune must be in want of a wife." How much credence she gave to the rumor was anyone's guess. This morning as she set off for Barnhouse, she was determined to keep an open mind about Donald Irish. She only wanted to ferret out some information about Leslie's mysterious new jockey. In truth, she felt a little absurd.

When the sun came up on this fine May morning, it had found Donald Irish already in the stable yard at Barnhouse. Leslie Downing was away on business, and in her absence Irish had taken it upon himself to supervise the staff. As her financial advisor, he considered it important to have a hand in things.

Irish was a tall man in his late forties, with thinning yellow hair. His expensive pinstripe suit looked rather out of place in the paddock. He was deep in conversation with a young stableboy of twelve or so, whose charges watched impassively from their boxes as a heated conversation took place.

"Really, Mr. Irish," the boy asserted, "I wasn't in the feed store. I promise."

"Now, Willy," said Donald Irish, "it's all right to make a mistake if you are big enough to admit to it." He glared at the boy. "Admit it, Willy, and we'll forget all about this episode." His tone was steely.

Willy let a sigh escape through compressed lips and lowered his eyes. Clearly, he was not going to win this one. He dug the toe of one sneaker viciously into the ground "Okay. I'm sorry."

"That's better. No harm done. Now back to work, and we won't say a word about this to Mrs. Downing."

Irish tugged fastidiously at the hem of his jacket and turned smartly toward the stables; Willy slouched off with a bad grace toward a little tack shed, muttering indignantly. Once inside the familiar room, with its warm smell of polished leather and mud, he snatched up a halter and a tin of saddle soap and set to work with a vengeance. "Stupid old guy," he said, sotto voce. "Don't *I* know if I been in the feed stores? Stupid. *She* would believe me."

A shadow fell across the tack room door. *"Ira furor brevis est,"* said Dewey James.

"Huh?" said Willy, looking up, his scowl deepening.

" 'Anger is a brief madness.' Horace."

"My name isn't Horace," said Willy.

"My mistake. Forgive me. I'm Mrs. James from down the road," she gestured vaguely behind her, "and I've come to return this." She held out a gap-toothed currycomb for Willy's inspection. He rose, wiping his hands on his jeans, as she continued. "Mrs. Downing was good enough to lend it to me the day that Starbuck had such terrible thistles in her tail, and I'm afraid it's taken me an age to return it. But here you go."

She handed it to Willy, who with a skeptical glance compared it to the array of well-cared-for brushes that lined his tack room shelves. He was clearly not pleased.

"Thanks." He dropped the seedy brush on the ground.

"Is Mrs. Downing here today?"

"No, ma'am. She's in Louisville. Till Friday."

"I see. And she naturally put you in charge while she's away."

This suggestion did much to make up for the raggedy currycomb. Willy swaggered slightly.

"Not *technically*, no. Hugh is here. We work together."

"Partners?"

"Kind of."

"Is Mr. Irish a partner, too?"

"Him?" Willy was incredulous.

"I see," said Dewey, who did see—a little bit, anyway. "Well!" she continued brightly, remembering her promise to George Farnham, "I was surprised to hear that Hugh won't be riding in the Hamilton Cup."

"He kinda didn't feel like it, I guess." Willy shrugged. "He's got a bad back."

"That's a pity. Rather closes a chapter of Barnhouse history, wouldn't you say?" Willy didn't respond. "Who will be up on Midnight Blue?" asked Dewey.

"Some new guy. Mark Gordon. He's gonna be a new trainer, and he just came last night. He'll do okay."

"That's not really the point, though, is it?"

Willy looked uneasy. "Uhh—listen, Mrs. James, I gotta get back to work." He held up the halter that he had been cleaning.

"Forgive me. Please tell Mrs. Downing I dropped by."

Dewey bustled out of the little tack shed and wandered toward a cluster of stable buildings, an expression of insouciance fixed firmly on her face. She turned in at the door of one of the stables, colliding with a tall man in a suit who looked decidedly out of place in these surroundings. She knew at once it was Donald Irish.

"Oh, I'm sorry!" exclaimed Dewey.

"Good morning. I'm afraid the stables are off-limits to visitors. Perhaps I can help you?"

Dewey sized the man up. His thin, yellowish hair had long ago begun a steady retreat from the front lines, and his suit jacket was distended somewhat across his belly. You couldn't actually call him fat, Dewey reflected, but there was a flabbiness about him that was distinctly unappealing. It struck her as a flabbiness of spirit, as much as of body. His face bore faint scars of bad adolescent acne, and his shiny nose was adorned with an inflorescence of tiny red lines and dots. His small, pinkish hands clutched a large buff envelope.

"You're Mr. Irish, aren't you? I'm Dewey James from down the road. I think we've met, actually, at Tommy O'Connor's going-away party."

"Forgive me, Mrs. James, of course, of course. I sometimes have trouble when there's a shift in context. You know—still trying to get to know everyone." He took her elbow and deftly guided her at a leisurely pace away from the stables. "Leslie's away on a little business, and I promised her I'd look in here from time to time, keep an eye on things. She'll be sorry to have missed you. But come and have some coffee if you like."

"Oh thank you, no, Mr. Irish. I'm—"

"Call me Donald."

"Donald, then—no thank you, I have miles of errands to run. I was just returning one of Leslie's currycombs. Well, it's not hers exactly, is it, for of course it belongs to the horses. I had a nice chat with the stableboy—"

"Willy?"

"Probably. I only know his name isn't Horace. The redhead in the tack house. I'm afraid that comb was *not* in very good shape when I gave it back to him, but he was too polite to say so. Nice boy."

"Mmm."

"But the thistles in Starbuck's tail were *so* dreadful that I broke my own—or her own, you know—and still they weren't out."

"Yes, well, glad to be of service."

They had arrived at Dewey's car, a dusty old station wagon whose rear window was adorned with several decals of enormous size and variety, all proclaiming the driver's unwavering support for the Hamilton Hornets.

"I see you are quite a fan," said Irish, indicating the decals.

"Oh, my, yes. I live for basketball season. We all do in Hamilton." She smiled sweetly. "You'll get used to our ways. Where did you move from, Mr. Irish?"

"Chicago. Had enough of big-city life, I suppose. And this job came up at the Warren, and I thought I'd give it a try."

"Well, I imagine it all still seems rather provincial to you—silly town fairs and high-school basketball. The Hornets, you know, benefit from the Hamilton Cup purse on Saturday."

"Yes, yes. So I've been told."

"I suppose, as a banker, you might think that the stables are throwing money away."

"Not at all, Mrs. James." He shook his head knowingly. "There is a lot to be said for creating good will."

"Right you are. Well." Dewey fished around for a way to ask her important question. "Thank you. And please thank Leslie for me. I guess I'll see her Saturday at the race."

"Oh, yes, she'll be back in plenty of time for the main event."

"This is your first time, isn't it, for the Hamilton Cup?"

"It is—but you know, I feel I've lived through it already somehow. Barnhouse is so geared up, and steeped in town tradition, and so forth." Irish looked a bit apologetic, as if aware of his unfortunate status as a newcomer. He was clearly determined to have as much fun as the old-timers. Dewey felt rather sorry for him.

"Well, it's bound to be a bit different this year. Too bad Hugh won't be riding. I hear Leslie is bringing in someone new." Dewey tried to sound casual.

"Town is probably abuzz with the news, eh?"

Dewey managed to look abashed, as though caught out in rumormongering. "Well, people do talk," she said, adopting an apologetic air of meekness that was often useful.

"Well, you can tell everyone that the new jockey's a fine fellow. His name is Mark Gordon, and we—that is, Leslie—is bringing him in as an assistant trainer. He'll be a fixture around the place by this time next year."

"Well!" said Dewey. "It won't be quite like old times—but then, a foolish consistency and all that. I'm off."

Irish held the door open for her with a rather appealing mixture of pride and diffidence. He was clearly pleased to be allowed to assume the role of host, however temporarily, at Barnhouse. As she headed out the driveway, Dewey thought perhaps that it surprised him, too, that Leslie Downing would show an interest in him. "Cupid is a knavish lad," she said to herself, as with a honk and a wave she tootled down the driveway.

Across the stable yard stood the small outbuilding that served as the Barnhouse business office. Within, the cheaply paneled walls were decorated with a haphazard group of photographs, documenting the series of noble horses that had passed through the remarkable hands of Leslie Downing. Against the far wall hung a calendar, the generous annual gift of Jensen's Feed and Grain to its regular customers. Somewhere along the line, Jensen's had grown tired of illustrations of crops; the current year's calendar offered, by way of an alternative, a rogue's gallery of insect pests. The May picture featured *Hypera nigrirostris*, the lesser cloverleaf weevil, in a revealing black-and-white portrait about thirty times life-size.

Seated at the old desk before the calendar, elbow-deep in papers, was Hugh Shields, Barnhouse's manager. He bent his grizzled head over a large, ruled ledger, and a puzzled look crossed his weathered features from time to time. Periodically he turned to the adding machine near his right hand—punch-punch-punch, click, click, chinka-ching!—and the puzzled expression would be gone, revealing clear blue eyes beneath strong brows. The machine was heavy and old; its Bakelite numbers rode high and proud on their posts, above a thick casing of dark gray steel. A long stream of paper, covered with figures, had inched its way out of the back of the machine. It now drooped in a lifeless stream toward the floor, like crepe paper after a party.

Hugh Shields took comfort in this machine, as he did in many of the old, tried-and-true fixtures of the office. Somehow this machine's assertions seemed right to him, or at least more believable than the vanishing figures that flickered across the solar panel of Donald Irish's sleek and silent calculator.

Irish. The man was beginning to get under Hugh's skin. He looked up in irritation at the second desk that had been installed in the cramped office. A halogen lamp sat pristinely on a sleek marble top. Irish's filing cabinet, always kept carefully locked, was of dark, matte steel that looked very expensive. Absurd. Italian pen-and-pencil set. More absurd still.

But the galling thing was that it had been Irish, with those stubby pink hands and fancy desk accessories; Irish, who didn't know a fetlock from a forelock, who had been able to turn Barnhouse around last season. Hugh and Leslie had come perilously close to losing everything; he had stepped in and saved them. Small wonder then that Leslie thought the world of him; Irish had preserved that world for her, intact. In so doing, he had insinuated himself neatly into it, and now he clung, like a moist limpet, to everything that Hugh Shields held dear.

Through the open door to the stable yard Hugh Shields watched with mounting irritation as Irish led dotty old Dewey James to her car and tucked her in carefully. The man was playing the host for all the world to see. As if he were the gentleman of the place. Hugh Shields sighed and told himself—as he did nearly every day now—that it couldn't last forever.

3

DONALD IRISH HAD been right: the little town of Hamilton was abuzz with the news that Hugh Shields had been unseated in the Hamilton Cup. Tongues wagged and eyebrows were raised and the matter was greatly discussed over pitchers of tavern beer and backyard lemonade alike. Nowhere was the subject more thoroughly examined than at that bastion of Hamiltonian style, the Tidal Wave Beauty Shop. Here, under the comforting influence of shampoos and lotions, in the lulling warmth of hair dryers, with the promises of various rinses before them, the ladies of Hamilton were wont to discuss important local affairs.

It was only natural, then, that Dewey James had secured an appointment with Doris Bock, proprietress of the Tidal Wave, at the earliest possible moment. Shortly after leaving Barnhouse she had telephoned the beauty parlor, and at eleven-thirty that morning she duly arrived.

"Is that you, Susan?" Dewey asked as she entered the shop. She addressed a semirecumbent figure whose face was shrouded by a limp, perfumed towel.

"Dewey! Hi!" came the muffled response. Susan Miles was one of Dewey's neighbors and an active member of civic circles in Hamilton. She was a good-looking mother of two small girls, and she and Dewey were close friends, despite the difference in their ages. In fact, Susan was rather touchingly devoted to Dewey. "I'm having a facial. How was California? How is Grace?"

"Grace is just marvelous, thank you," Dewey replied. "I

think that there is something exotic about California, even in these tired modern days. All those palm trees, you know, and avocados and things."

"And the good-looking men in sports cars," laughed Doris, as she seated Dewey before the shampooing sink. "Now, Mrs. James, how about the full treatment today?"

"Just my usual wash and set, thanks, Doris," said Dewey, as she submitted to being draped in a large red apron.

"Dewey, have you heard the news about Hugh and the point-to-point?" called Susan.

"Indeed I have," Dewey called back over the noise of the running faucets. "I wonder if perhaps he's not well?"

"He's perfectly fine—except of course tremendously down in the dumps, I guess," Susan replied.

Little Mary Barstow, the hygienist at the local dental clinic, sat beneath a huge old-fashioned dryer, flipping impatiently through the tired pages of a worn fashion magazine. Her forehead was pink with heat, almost matching the color of the soft curlers that held her black hair.

"I think Leslie's trying to squeeze him out," said Mary, looking up briefly. "I think she's a cold fish. How she could make poor Hugh unhappy, after all these years, that—"

"Now, Mary, you don't know for sure. Maybe Hugh didn't want to ride," came Susan's voice from under her towel.

"If you had seen him the other day, when he came in to see Doctor Langford, you'd know he was upset."

"I always turn green when I go to see Doctor Langford," pointed out Doris Bock. Her tone was official; she liked to direct conversation in the shop, and was apt to put a stop to talk she considered unwise or unprofitable. Or dull.

"But I can tell when it's just nerves from the dentist," pursued Mary. "It's part of my job to know that. Besides, Hugh has great teeth. Never a problem."

"What's his secret, I wonder?" asked Susan.

"Flossing," said Mary. "If every one of Doctor Langford's patients would only—"

"You're *so* right, Mary," Doris interrupted, sparing them all this familiar homily on the virtues of dental floss. "Now, Mrs.

James, if you'll just come this way." She led Dewey to a chair before a large mirror.

Dewey pursued her subject. "Hugh really has been the heart and soul of Barnhouse for years. Do you think Leslie is trying to force him out, Susan?"

"He's not young anymore, that's for certain," replied Susan. "But I think it has to do with Donald Irish."

"But he knows nothing about thoroughbreds," put in Mary.

"He seems to have Leslie wrapped around his little finger," replied Susan. "And she's a thoroughbred if there ever was one."

The ladies mused awhile on this point, and no one disagreed.

"I think it's a shame about Hugh," said Dewey. "The whole situation reminded me somehow of—well, something's not quite right there, you know. Perhaps Barnhouse is having financial troubles." She settled herself into her seat and looked appraisingly at her reflection in the mirror. Doris began to comb Dewey's hair out.

"Well, of *course* it is; everyone knows that. But what business isn't these days?" asked Doris. The question provoked an awkward momentary silence; Doris had just last week raised prices at the Tidal Wave.

Doris stuck enormous flat clips in Dewey's hair, clamping her gray curls firmly in place, and began to dab at them with a greenish goopy gel.

"Doris, what *is* that confection you are putting on me?" Dewey demanded.

"It's the latest thing, Mrs. James. Hair polisher." Doris held up a tiny jar for Dewey's inspection. "Makes you shine."

"Doris, I don't want to shine. I just want to look presentable."

Doris smiled, and Susan Miles giggled under her towel. Making Dewey presentable was easy; but unfortunately the effects rarely lasted more than a few brief hours. In no time, Dewey would be digging rosebushes in her garden, or tossing a pitchfork full of hay to her seedy mare, or shaking the dust of ages from books in the storeroom at the library. Dewey lived too heartily to have time for the niceties of coiffure.

"Leslie was having problems last fall," put in Susan Miles, "or at least I think so."

"How do you know?" asked Mary Barstow.

"I saw her in the bank, and I think she was there to ask for a loan."

Everyone leaned forward eagerly. "Well?" someone asked.

Susan sat up and removed her towel, conscious of her rapt audience. "I was there one day, to put the fire insurance policy away in the safe deposit. And you know how Tommy O'Connor used to have that glass-walled office. Like a fishbowl. Which I always thought was perfect because he is sort of fishy-looking."

"Wall-eyed, like a pike," agreed Doris.

"Maybe that's it. And I saw Leslie Downing talking to him. She looked really angry."

"When was this?" asked Mary.

"In September, maybe. Yes—it was September. Nicholas and I finished the addition to the house in August, but we didn't get around to adjusting the policy for a couple of weeks because Milton was away on vacation." Milton Shoemaker was one of the local insurance agents.

"How do you know Leslie was asking for a loan?"

"I don't, really—but she left at about the same time I did, and Hugh was waiting for her in the Jeep out front. And as she got in she said, 'I have just been informed that Meretricious and Stanley Steamer aren't worth their weight in oats.' Or something like that."

"And that was *just* before Donald Irish was transferred to town," Doris Bock put in. "Tommy left in October, I think."

"Well, well—now we know why the big romance got off the ground, anyway," put in Mary. Silence followed this remark. It was the received wisdom of Hamilton that Mary herself might once have been inclined to set her cap for Donald Irish. But Leslie Downing had eclipsed her chances.

"Now, Mary. We don't know any such thing," asserted Doris Bock. "Her spending so much time with him may have nothing to do with money."

"Or if she did get a loan from Warren State, it might be

because Irish understands the monetary value of race horses better than Tommy O'Connor."

"Or the monetary value of *something*, anyway," said Mary acidly.

"Mary!" reproved Doris. Her cheeks crimson, Mary retreated beneath the hood of the enormous dryer and turned the setting up. The machine roared.

"Well, I for one will be interested to see how the new trainer does," said Dewey. "They tell me he has quite a record—and there must be a reason that Leslie is bringing him in."

"But Mrs. James," put in Doris, "it's certainly not necessary for him to ride in the point-to-point. There's no purse, really, and it's *our* race, not some professional thing."

"I agree, Doris," said Susan Miles. "Leslie Downing is sending a message. Poor Hugh." She glanced at Mary, who was apparently absorbed in her reading, and stage-whispered to Dewey, "But the Lord only knows what she sees in that degenerate-looking banker. He's so—so—*pinkish*, if you know what I mean."

"I do," agreed Dewey, with a hasty nod toward Mary. It was difficult to be sure she couldn't hear them.

"News of the romance seems to have traveled far and wide, anyway," said Doris. "I hear the prodigal son is returning for the race."

"Peter Downing?" asked Dewey. "He was at Hamilton High with Grace. I always thought him charming, but Brendan couldn't abide him. Refused to let Grace go to the school dance with him one year."

"Wasn't that the year he drove his car into the side of the gym?"

"Yes. And poor Marlese Gilbert came home at three A.M. with a broken collarbone."

"Peter hasn't been home to Hamilton in years," said Susan in a speculative tone. "The affair must be serious. I wonder if he's coming to check on the romantic angle or the business angle?"

"Leslie Downing would be quite a catch for that man," said Doris. "She's awfully attractive."

"And even if Barnhouse is having problems, she's still the

biggest property owner for sixty miles. As rich as Cronos," added Susan, "which will make Irish happy."

"*Croesus*, dear," corrected Dewey gently, "Croesus. You know: 'Account no man happy before his death,' and all that."

An hour later Dewey, still aglow with hair polisher, mounted the long flight of granite steps that led up to the portico of the Grain Merchants' Exchange. The huge Greek Revival building had once been the center of fevered trade; a century ago, Hamilton had been at the hub of important railway routes traveling west and north. The trains were long gone, and with them much of the activity that had made Hamilton flourish; but the imposing building was still the center of town life. It housed the county clerk's office, as well as two courtrooms and the mayor's office.

As town council president, George Farnham kept a small office here, too, in the garretlike precincts of the fourth floor. Dewey climbed three flights of stairs and made her way down a narrow hallway, along an allée of sturdy oak doors, to George's office. His door stood open; Dewey knocked softly and entered.

"Hello, George. I was passing by and thought I'd report my findings. Meager as they are."

"Dewey!" cried the delighted George, leaping up from his chair. "My dear, let me take you to lunch and hear all."

"You don't need to buy me lunch, George. You must have a ton of things to do."

"Nothing as important as having a grilled cheese sandwich with you. You may have *two* grilled cheeses, if you like. Will Josie's Place suit?"

"Perfectly, thank you."

"Good. Let's away." He took his jacket down from its peg and ushered her briskly out the door.

Josie's Place was, in its way, as central to life in Hamilton as the Grain Merchants' Building. An eccentric cross between a family diner and a full-blown restaurant, it was a favorite with all Hamiltonians. In the comfort of Josie's well-worn chairs, they dined on home-style cooking of a superior sort. Josie herself had presided over this cheerful groaning board for nearly half a century, perfecting her mastery of chipped beef, steaks, fried chicken, and pies, while resolutely ignoring the rising and falling tides of *le ton cuisiniere*.

As their sandwiches arrived, Dewey related to George the events of the morning, beginning with her tale of the stable-boy's distress, and ending with the conversation at the Tidal Wave.

"George, I have never seen anything as beautifully organized and cared for as that tack shed. Willy takes great pride, it's clear, in doing his job well."

"Therefore?" asked George, biting down on his turkey club.

"Well—therefore, I think something is amiss at Barnhouse." Dewey poked at her grilled cheese sandwich.

"I don't follow you, Dewey."

"It's just that I can't see there is anything wrong with the way Hugh manages things. And he's such a nice man. But Donald Irish was very upset with young Willy."

"You say Susan Miles thinks the problems are financial."

"That's true, she does. But the kind of trouble I mean is in the daily operation of the place. In the chores."

"Dewey, the boy is surely not infallible. He must have made some kind of mistake."

"Mistakes are the portals of discovery, George."

George laughed. "A genius's mistakes, my dear. I doubt your earnest redhead is a genius. Did you talk to Hugh?"

"No, I didn't see him at all. He must have been in the office. I didn't want to go poking around. And that Donald Irish did not want me in the stables. I don't like the way he watched me with those bulgy eyes of his."

"Exophthalmic. Maybe you should talk to Leslie."

"I can't do that, George, really I can't. Especially if she's in love with the man."

"I suppose not." He popped the last bite of his pickle into his mouth. "I guess there's nothing anyone can do except wait and see."

"We can talk to Hugh on Saturday, after the race."

"You're right. By then, everyone will have calmed down considerably."

"Yes." Dewey bit heartily into her sandwich.

4

By THE FOLLOWING day, Dewey had settled back into her household routine. The effects of Doris Bock's hair polisher, if in truth there had been any, were a thing of the past. The concerns of Leslie Downing and her entourage vanished, too, as Dewey went about her busy life.

She was officially semiretired from her work as the town librarian, but she liked to look in most days at the Hamilton Free Library to be sure things were running smoothly. In fact, she detested the notion of being "semiretired." She admitted the practicality of the arrangement, but she loathed the terminology.

"How can you be 'semiretired,' George?" she had asked one day in a fit of annoyance, shortly before resigning her full-time duties. "It's absurd. Either you do a thing, or you don't do it. Must women be half-workers?" But she was obliged to own, in moments of candid conversation with herself, that she was sometimes just a little tired at the end of a full day.

This afternoon, as she headed for home in her dusty old station wagon, Dewey's mind was in the stacks—specifically, in the Mystery & Suspense section, from which several volumes had disappeared. Discovery of the thefts had provoked much discussion because the missing books were new acquisitions and the book-buying budget was small. Tom Campbell, the new librarian, had begun to insist on security tags for all the books, and the installation of an alarm at the door.

Dewey was firmly opposed. Her beloved books were not

meant for such garish technology; nor would security measures really protect the collection. Those who wanted to steal would find a way around it and would not hesitate to destroy the spines. Then the books would be not only missing, but ruined.

So Dewey was trying to work out another plan. She thought she might even know the identity of one or two culprits; she reasoned that involvement in the library's activities would do much to dampen the impulse to steal. Her opinions, however, were regarded skeptically by Tom Campbell. He was a curious combination of pomposity and innocence, and Dewey thought him an idiot. But a nice idiot.

Campbell held that any "soft arrangement" (as he phrased it) would only provide greater opportunity for theft. He was a self-proclaimed law-and-order man, and liked to perorate on the subject of "interdiction." Thus Dewey's first day back on the job had been trying.

So absorbed was Dewey in her thoughts that she had driven a full mile out of town before she remembered an important errand—Starbuck's feed order. Checking the road carefully for the state trooper's yellow sedan, she made an illegal U-turn and headed back, pulling up in front of Jensen's Feed & Grain.

As Dewey entered the shop, a little bell above the door tinkled, and she was greeted with the dusty but comforting smell of gardening and farm merchandise. The powdery scent of lime and phosphorus mingled agreeably with the warmth of peat moss. The effect was solid and reassuring, and reminiscent of Saturday mornings.

"Afternoon, Mrs. James!" called Rob Jensen from behind the counter. "Be with you in a minute." With a look of patient annoyance the proprietor returned his attention to the customer who stood before him. It was Donald Irish. Dewey sidled over to the rack of corn-seed packets and gave them her earnest attention. She was all ears.

"That's right, Mr. Irish, fifty pounds of oats. Fifty's what they weight in at, and what we sell. We sell you oats."

"That's all very well, Mr. Jensen, but I should like to have a look, anyway, if you don't mind."

"I do mind. Now, Mr. Irish. Hugh's got a standing order with us for delivery every month. If you think there's something wrong with the feed, the problem must be at Barnhouse. But I think," he continued, breathing in impressively, "that you must be mistaken. And I will ask you kindly to speak to me, in future, and not to my men. I trust them both, and so should you."

"We'll have to see about that, won't we?" said Donald Irish smoothly. He turned and stalked out of the shop, nodding to Dewey as he passed.

"How do you do, Mr. Jensen?" began Dewey politely, as she stepped up to the counter. "I hope you are well."

"How do, Mrs. James," returned the merchant. "I'm afraid I'm in for a bit of a tussle with that one." He nodded in the direction of the door.

"Nothing serious, I hope?"

"No, no." But Jensen's face belied this simple assurance.

"I gather he has taken rather an interest in the success of Barnhouse," said Dewey in a leading fashion.

"That's true enough," replied Jensen. "He says, you know, that there's a problem with the feed."

"Well, we know that's not possible," said Dewey politely.

"I hear he wants to place their standing order with some direct-mail fellows, with a computer and a fax machine."

"How very forward-looking of him."

Rob Jensen cocked an appreciative eyebrow at this bit of irony.

"But between you and me, Mrs. James, that man wouldn't know a sack of oats if it fell on him."

"Is that so?" Dewey was interested. "I wonder, then, why he comes to see you himself?"

"Likes to have his finger in the pie, my guess. Next he'll be training the horses." Jensen shook his head.

"I hear there are some changes underway at Barnhouse," murmured Dewey. "A new assistant trainer who is going to ride in the Hamilton Cup." She shook her head meaningfully.

"Strange," agreed Jensen. "His idea, no doubt." He nodded toward the door.

"Well, perhaps Hugh feels he's getting a bit long in the tooth for racing."

"I don't know about that. Hugh was out on Midnight Blue

last week, running over the course. I think I know whose idea this new trainer was. And I expect it'll take more brains than Irish has to get around old Hugh Shields."

Rob Jensen was a well-liked and quiet Swede, on the whole rather disinclined to gossip. His observations, therefore, came as a surprise to Dewey. She realized that the rifts in Hamilton society were beginning to run very deep indeed. The goings-on at Barnhouse were now clearly more than grist for the Tidal Wave's gossip mill. They were an issue.

"Oh, I'm sure that Mrs. Downing will restore order when she returns," Dewey responded.

"Maybe," mused Jensen, "and then again, maybe not."

"Well. I've just come to order this month's feed," said Dewey, rummaging in her capacious handbag for her checkbook. The two embarked on a lively discussion of Starbuck's needs, debating the virtues of various brands of feed designed for aging horses. Amused, Dewey ordered up two fifty-pound bags of something called "Old Gray Mare," commenting with a smile that she might try a bowlful herself for breakfast. And with a presence of mind that astonished her, Dewey remembered to buy a new currycomb for Starbuck. Then she was on her way.

As she drove home through the late spring afternoon, Dewey thought over the scene she had just witnessed. It had disturbed and puzzled her. Was Hamilton really such a closed little society? For it appeared to Dewey that her neighbors were closing ranks against Irish.

Why? Because he was a newcomer? A little gauche, a little unused to their ways? He hadn't quite got the hang of things yet, hadn't developed the nonchalance—or was it the *sang froid*—of most Hamiltonians. But who had given the poor man a chance? In fact, Leslie Downing seemed to be his only friend in Hamilton. Surely that spoke of small-mindedness.

By the time she got home, Dewey was thoroughly ashamed of herself. Wasn't Leslie Downing entitled to run her business—as well as her love life, if it came to that—in any way she liked? Dewey was mortified by her part in the gossipy chase. It seemed almost like a witch-hunt to her, so eager were they all to find fault with Irish. He wasn't a very sympathetic character, Dewey reflected; he seemed ungenerous and self-important. But what of it, really?

Dewey resolved to go no further in these ridiculous inquiries; and her resolution made her feel briefly virtuous. But she knew that the almost prurient interest which the other townsfolk took in the matter would not be so quick to flag. Currycomb in hand, Dewey picked her way across the small field toward Starbuck's stall, greeting her old friend with a sad-sounding hello. "Oh, Starbuck," said Dewey, producing half an apple from her pocket, "we are a pernicious race of little odious vermin."

5

ON THURSDAY MORNING, Peter Downing poured himself a glass of orange juice in the old-fashioned kitchen at Barnhouse. A tall, lanky, handsome man in his early thirties, he had blue eyes and dark brown hair that swept charmingly down over his forehead. He moved about the familiar country kitchen easily, with the lithe grace of the natural athlete and a quiet self-assurance that was an echo of his mother's style.

He sipped at his juice abstractedly, staring out the window to the well-remembered fields and buildings beyond, with a look of annoyance on his face. He had flown in from Chicago yesterday to find out how things stood at Barnhouse, and what he had learned thus far did not please him.

Last night, Peter had called at the small stone tenant's cottage on the other side of the paddock, where Hugh Shields lived. For years there had been a kind of armed truce between them. Hugh resented Peter's decision to leave Barnhouse for a law practice in Chicago. But Peter, with all his faults, represented the old order at Barnhouse, and Hugh was glad on that account that he had come to call.

Neither man had much use for cordial preliminaries, so after a few words of greeting, Peter got to the point.

"How far has it gone, Hugh?"

"What do you mean, 'gone'?"

"Come off it. You know what I'm talking about. All I know about this man Irish is what my mother has told me. And that, you can imagine, is not much. I gather there's some kind of an understanding."

"That's an old-fashioned word for romance, Peter."

"My mother is not a romantic woman."

"Right you are."

"Well?"

"Peter, I work for your mother. Don't ask me to judge her personal life. She's entitled."

"But is *he*?"

Hugh was silent for a moment. Then he seemed to come to a decision. He stood up and reached for a bottle of single-malt whiskey, throwing Peter a questioning look.

"Sure, thanks. On the rocks."

Hugh shook his head. There was much that was lacking in Peter Downing's character. Diluting good whiskey with ice cubes spoke volumes. Hugh shambled over to the tiny kitchen. "Tall glass?" he called.

"No, just a small one."

Hugh returned, ice clinking in Peter's glass. He poured out two small dollops of the ginger-colored liquid and returned to his seat.

"Here you go."

"Thanks. Cheers." Peter took a small sip and waited.

He had known Hugh Shields since childhood, since the days when his father had still been around. If Hugh wanted to talk, he would tell things in his own way, at his own pace. As an impatient young boy, Peter had often been infuriated by this mannerism: Hugh would take ages to answer a simple question about taking a fence, or training a horse. The child Peter had thought it conceit, or a need to make mysteries of simple things.

He remembered now a scene between the two of them, the week after Peter's father left. It was October, early in the morning, and they had gone out riding together. This in itself was an unusual occurrence, for Hugh was generally too busy managing the fledgling business at the stables to have much time for his employer's small son.

They had ridden as far as the ridge of Adams Hill, and from there they looked at the rolling green countryside, just beginning to be touched by the colors of fall. The air was sharp and cool, but it was still early. It would be a fine, warm Indian summer day.

They had sat in silence for a long time, and finally Peter had steeled himself to utter the question he couldn't put to his mother.

"Why did he go, Hugh?" Peter had asked in a small voice, half-hoping he wouldn't be heard. He had asked; it wouldn't be his fault if nobody answered.

By way of a response, Hugh nodded toward the horizon, where two streams merged to make a small river. Four miles downriver, beyond what they could see, was a cliff. There, the mingled waters tumbled precipitously down a sheer forty-foot drop.

"Maybe he didn't like to think what might lie ahead," said Hugh, turning his horse and setting off for home in a gallop.

This oracular answer had made Peter furious. He became convinced that Hugh knew more than he was telling, and for months he had waited, suspended, for himself and his mother to rush headlong over that fatal cliff. But as he grew older, and as life at Barnhouse went on, unchanged but more intense, Peter had grown to appreciate Hugh's obscurity. He was thankful both for its accuracy and for the scope it allowed his own imagination.

Now, drinking whiskey in the man's small sitting room, Peter was content to hear this new story in Hugh's words and to let his own mind interpret such facts as came his way.

"I don't think she's in love with him," Hugh finally said, "but she's in love with what he can do." He looked up at Peter. "We were in a jam. Bought what we shouldn't have, borrowed too much money at too high interest rates. At one point it looked like your mother might have to sell off about seventy-five acres to that real-estate developer who's building condominiums. Two foals died, another was lame. A catastrophe."

"And? What did he do?"

"He's a numbers man, Peter. He came in, looked at the books, gave your mother a loan, and did some fancy accounting. In six months we were almost back on our feet."

"I see."

"He saved Barnhouse for her."

"And well we know that Barnhouse is the only thing she cares for." Peter's tone was acid. "Is she going to marry him?"

Hugh stood up and moved to the window, looking out onto the paddock in the soft, moonlit glow. "I can't say. She hasn't confided in me."

Peter heard the disappointment in Hugh's voice, and for the first time seemed to realize the effect that Irish's ascendancy must be having on him. He wondered how old Hugh was— fifty-five? Sixty? Probably. He had been about thirty when he came to work for Peter's mother; he had been good-looking and strong. When Peter's father left, some of the town wags had chalked it up to the influence of the handsome new manager. Peter wondered idly if there had ever been anything more than friendship between Hugh and his mother.

There was an awkward silence in the small room. Peter, conscious of his sudden redundancy, rose. "Gotta sleep," he said, clapping Hugh on the shoulder. "Thanks for the drink. And for filling me in."

"Yep," said Hugh. "You should come back here, you know."

Peter laughed politely. At least this old quarrel was safe ground between the two of them. "I can't stand the sight of horses, Hugh." He headed out into the night, across the paddock, to the waiting, darkened farmhouse that had been his childhood home.

Now, drinking his juice in the brightly lighted kitchen, Peter reviewed this scene in his mind. His mother was due back today from Louisville. He planned a little confrontation when she returned. There was something going on here that he didn't like. He would get to the bottom of it, one way or another.

6

WILLY WAS STILL angry with Donald Irish, but he was determined that the man would not spoil tomorrow for him. Even at eleven years of age Willy was enough of a professional to overcome bad feelings when they got in the way of pleasurable duty. Tomorrow would be a day of great excitement and of particular glory for Willy himself. Ordinarily the professional stable hands readied the horses for a race; but the Hamilton Cup, by Barnhouse tradition, belonged to the youngest stable hand. Tomorrow belonged to Willy.

He straightened the row of brushes and combs on the small shelf in the tack shed and thought about what was to come. In the early morning, he would feed and water Midnight Blue, then lead him out into the north enclosure for a short period of exercise. As the time for the race approached, Midnight's bridle and saddle—gleaming with the luster imparted by Willy's ministrations—would be brought from the tack house. The magnificent scarlet blanket, emblazoned with the Barnhouse crest and the number 13, had been draped carefully over a hook in the corner tonight. Tomorrow it would catch the light as Midnight speeded over the countryside, lifting himself with a glorious greatness over the brush fences and water jumps of the familiar course.

Willy allowed himself a momentary regret that Hugh would not be riding; this was the only tarnish on tomorrow's brilliant prospect. The thought soon was dispelled. The new trainer didn't matter at all; he was only along for the ride. Midnight Blue, Willy knew, would be perfection itself.

He took up Midnight's bridle and a tin of saddle soap and lovingly began to rub and polish it once more. Outside, darkness had fallen. The glow of a kerosene lamp in the corner brought a further sense of adventure and excitement to Willy's preparations.

When the bridle could not be made to shine any brighter, Willy glanced at his wristwatch and resigned himself to going home. It was nearly nine-thirty, and he had promised his parents that he would be in bed by ten o'clock. They had stubbornly refused him permission to spend the night at Barnhouse. Naturally Willy had argued his case well, citing the many unprofessional aspects of their decision. What if he were needed in the night? But his arguments had not won the day. He put out the lamp.

With a last look behind him, Willy gently closed and locked the door and climbed on his bicycle. He would take a shortcut across the south enclosure; the fences were being mended, and even in the dark Willy knew where the gaps were. Above him, raggedy clouds chased across the face of the moon. Glancing up, Willy made a silent plea for fine weather. Then he headed off down the long Barnhouse drive, just as the wind began to rise behind him.

Alone in a small, fieldstone tenant's cottage—his home of thirty years—Hugh Shields poured himself a stiff shot of single-malt whiskey and listened as the wind came up, banging the shutters of his little house. A pocket-sized, spiral-bound notebook, bearing a few isolated notations, absorbed all his attention. *CK co? Security. s.p.—list? reit.* And something that looked like *uccls.* The book was otherwise empty of information. He turned it over, shaking out the pages. Nothing fell out. He turned again to the notes made on the last page, sipping gently at his whiskey.

He stared out into space for a time, letting the book drop with a flopping noise onto the desk. The puzzled expression remained firmly on his face. But eventually, with a look of resolution in his eyes, he drained off the last of the whiskey in his glass and reached for his Windbreaker.

* * *

Snug in her small parlor, deep in the welcoming embrace of a red armchair, Dewey James was sipping a cup of tea. A book lay open in her lap; it was *Macbeth*.

Isaiah, snoring at Dewey's feet, whimpered in his sleep. Dewey gave a start. The wind was rising noisily outside, and she wondered if she should look in on Starbuck, but decided against it. She really must be on her guard against such compulsive behavior. Time to go to sleep.

"Come on, you black monster," Dewey said, rising. Isaiah looked at her and yawned hugely. "Ope not thy ponderous and marble jaws, Ophelia, but get thee to a nunnery." The dog shot her a look full of disdain. He knew what was coming. She led the reluctant Isaiah to the back door and opened it wide for him. He gave her a parting doleful glance and moved toward his cozy doghouse with a painful slowness, as though suddenly stricken with the gout. Dewey looked up at the brightly moonlit sky, which was filling with clouds. The wind blew sharply, sending needles of wintry cold through the interstices of her purple sweater. She shivered, gathering that redoubtable garment closer around her, then bolted the door and headed for bed.

The horses were dozing dreamily in their stalls when the stable door opened gently. There came a series of soft, quiet footsteps. The beam of a flashlight picked out hard-packed earth scattered with hay. The torch beam shone momentarily on the long, powerful nose of Midnight Blue, who regarded his visitor impassively and let out a small snort.

Then the footsteps retreated, the door was closed once more, and all was quiet.

7

"COME ON, MOM, forget it, please. Please?"

"Willy, I want you to eat something," said Louisa Grimes in a stern voice. Her eyes were still half-closed with drowsiness, and her bright red hair stood out in alarming disarray. Nonetheless, she was remarkably pretty.

"Just give me a piece of toast. I promise I'll be okay. Please, Mom, I'm gonna be late."

"Listen to your mother, Willy." Jack Grimes sympathized with his son, but it wouldn't do to have an argument.

Willy was dressed and ready to go, but the rest of the family were still in their pajamas. They had all risen extremely early to see him off on his big day. Jack and Louisa hated to get up early.

"Toast will do, Willy. Sit down while I make it for you."

Willy sat, kicking his chair impatiently and looking at his watch every ten seconds while the toast was being made. His mother placed a glass of juice before him. "Drink up."

"Mom," Willy protested.

"Willy's gonna get in trouble!" chattered a small girl delightedly. This was Hannah, incorrigible at seven years of age. Willy rolled his eyeballs at her and stuck out his tongue.

"Enough from the peanut gallery, young lady," said Jack Grimes. "Willy, don't make faces at your sister."

"Yes sir." Willy and Hannah giggled. Hannah kicked him under the table. He kicked her back.

"Stop it, you two." Louisa Grimes was in no mood for her children this morning.

"What are you gonna do, Willy?" asked Hannah. "Do we get to see you on the horse?"

Willy sighed patiently. He had explained it all to her several times, but she refused to pay attention. "No, dodo-head. I am getting Midnight ready for the race."

"But the race is later!"

"There is a lot to do," said Willy importantly. "Mom, can I go?"

"Finish your toast."

"I'll take it with me. Okay?" He looked at his watch again.

"Yes. Fine. Go." Louisa kissed him. "We love you. We'll see you at the race."

"Don't fall off the horse!" shrieked Hannah. Then she collapsed in a fit of giggles in her chair.

Willy biked as fast as his legs would go. The sun had not yet risen, but he wanted more than anything to be the first person on the scene at Barnhouse this morning. It was nearly five-thirty; the grooms would be at the stable by six. Willy pedaled like a maniac and was turning in the driveway a mere seven minutes later. He roared up to the stable yard, out of breath but enormously happy. He looked at his watch: twelve minutes. A record.

He paused a minute to catch his breath, then opened the door to the small stable where Midnight Blue was lodged. It was still dark inside, and Willy groped for the light switch. Even as he did so, he had the sense that there was something wrong. From Midnight's box there came a labored breathing, followed by a whinny.

The lights flashed on. Willy looked around. There was no one here—but in the farthest stall was Midnight Blue, a picture of equine distress. His ears were flattened back completely, and his eyes looked wildly at Willy. Then he gave a furious whinny.

Willy glanced around at the three other horses in the stable. Midnight's mood had caught on; they all gazed at Willy with frightened eyes. But Midnight was the worst of the bunch.

"Midnight, old fella. It's me. What's wrong?" Willy sauntered over to the stallion's box and reached out a hand. The horse reared and let out a loud snort.

"Hey, hey, Midnight." Willy reached over the rail, and as the horse came down on his forelegs the boy managed to grab the halter. "Whoa, boy, easy now. Easy, boy, easy." He clucked at the horse, stroking his nose. Midnight would not be comforted. His eyes bulged with terror and he strained fiercely as Willy struggled to hold on to the halter. "What's up, boy?"

Willy climbed on the rail and looked down into the stall. Donald Irish lay on the hard earth floor, sprawled unnaturally, his eyes blank and staring. There was a thin brown line running from his temple down along his cheek to his jaw.

For a moment, Willy had no idea what he was seeing. Then he looked at Midnight, and saw again the terror in the horse's eyes. There was now an answering terror in his own. Willy forced himself to be calm as the blood pounded in his head. His hands felt like ice and his heart raced. Holding tight to the halter with one hand, Willy groped for the catch to the stall door. He managed to get it open, talking to the stallion in a soft, constant, reassuring voice, coaxing him out. "Steady, Midnight. That's a good boy. Steady, boy, easy." It took a great deal of strength and all of Willy's concentration, but he managed to lead the horse out through the stable and into a nearby enclosure.

Then Willy took off, running with all his might, and calling at the top of his lungs for Hugh Shields.

8

IT WAS EARLY Saturday morning, and the sky was a pale blue.
Whatever storm had threatened last night had blown away, and
the winds had brought in their place a lofty ceiling of clear air.
Poor-looking remnants of cloud were zooming about overhead
as Dewey made her way out past Isaiah's doghouse to
Starbuck's little stall. Dewey had a big day ahead of her. The
library guild was having a tailgate picnic at Barnhouse before
the race, and Dewey had promised to bring two dozen deviled
eggs.

"What a glorious day," she remarked aloud. Starbuck
greeted her mistress with a strong nudge in the shoulder. "Yes,
hello, you silly horse," said Dewey gently, stroking the mare's
velvety nose. "You silly, beautiful horse."

Behind her, Dewey heard the sound of wheels in the driveway. She turned, surprised to see George Farnham's car appear
around the little bend. She went to meet him.

"George! You're an early bird!"

"Hello, Dewey." George's face was pale and full of concern.

"What is it?"

He climbed out of the car. "Bad news, I'm afraid. It's
Donald Irish. There was some kind of accident at Barnhouse
last night, and he's dead."

"Dead!"

"Your young stableboy found him this morning when he got
to the stalls, just before dawn."

"This is terrible news," Dewey said gravely. "Terrible. How is Leslie?" They moved off toward the house.

"Well, Charlie O'Donovan has been to see her, gave her a little sedative. Hugh called me first thing to discuss postponing the race. I'm supposed to help get the word out. It's off, I'm afraid, at least for now."

"Yes, I suppose it would be. Well, come in and tell me all about it."

They made their way into the house through the kitchen door. As Dewey made a pot of coffee, George told her the details of Willy's grisly discovery.

"Brave Willy!" said Dewey proudly. "But what was Donald Irish doing there?"

"No idea. But he must have spooked that stallion. It looks like the horse dealt him a nasty blow to the temple."

"Oh, this is terrible. They're sure to kill him."

"Kill whom?"

"Midnight Blue, of course. Come on, George, hurry up." Dewey reached for George's coffee cup and put it in the sink. Then she donned her indispensable purple sweater and grabbed her handbag off the back of a chair. "Come *on*."

The startled George leaped to his feet and followed quickly.

In less than ten minutes they had arrived at Barnhouse. Everything looked quiet, but there was a feeling of suspended business about the place, like the calm right after a tornado has passed, before the losses are counted. Dewey recognized a car in the driveway as belonging to Tack Marvin, the local veterinarian. George's car came to a halt next to the old stable building. Dewey leaped out and ran in a burst of speed for the door.

In Midnight's stable, the air was anything but calm. The morning light came in softly through the door, but the overhead lights were still on. Hugh Shields sat, looking utterly defeated, on an upturned crate in a corner, his head in his hands. Peter Downing leaned up against one of the stall doors, hands in his pockets, watching the scene. Willy, his face dirty and tearstained, held center stage. He was protesting loudly to a round, balding, middle-aged man who held a menacing-looking hypodermic syringe in one hand.

"I don't *care*! I'll look after him, I *will*, please!" Willy held the man's left arm tight, pulling it toward his chest.

"Willy," said Hugh Shields in a dull voice. "Boy, there's nothing we can do about it."

"Young man, I appreciate your concern—" the vet began.

"No you *don't*!" Willy's voice was rising shrilly. "You're a *murderer*!" Willy kicked at the man savagely.

"Ahem."

The group noticed Dewey and George for the first time.

"Hello, Hugh," she said. "Good morning, everyone. I am so sorry to hear about this terrible tragedy."

"Morning, Mrs. James," Dr. Marvin responded. "It is terrible, you are right about that." He looked again at Willy, his face full of concern.

"He's gonna kill Midnight!" Willy burst out, looking ready to cry again.

"Just get it over with, man," said Peter Downing in a strange voice.

"Doctor Marvin, if I might have a word with you?" Dewey gestured to the door. The vet looked surprised but was obviously glad of this momentary reprieve from the operatic emotions of the young stable hand. He stepped outside with Dewey.

"Doctor, is there a law that requires you to take this step right away?"

"No, ma'am, there isn't," admitted the doctor. "It's usually easier on all concerned, however, to get this kind of thing over with."

"I understand that. But let me see if I have the facts in the case. Mr. Irish must have entered the stable at some point in the night, and gone into Midnight's stall? Is that right?"

"It appears so. The doctor who examined him said he had been dead about six to twelve hours. There was a severe blow to the head. I found traces of blood on the animal's left fore. The horse must have been spooked. No fault of his, of course, but there it is. And he kicked Irish and Irish was killed. The horse will have to be put down, Mrs. James."

Dewey reflected briefly. "Do you—could I ask for a brief

stay of execution, Doctor?" She looked at the veterinarian seriously, with no glint of humor in her eyes.

"Mrs. James, I'm afraid that won't do anybody any good."

"Perhaps not. But I understand that Mrs. Downing is in somewhat of a state of shock. And it doesn't look to me as though Hugh is in any shape to make this kind of decision for her this morning. Perhaps if we could have forty-eight hours to consider the case."

The vet scratched his head. He still clutched the huge syringe in his hand, and now he regarded the instrument with detachment. Then he looked back toward the stable, where Willy's sobs were punctuated by low-toned comments from Hugh. Peter Downing suddenly appeared on the threshold of the old building.

"Doctor?" he called, in a peremptory tone.

"I will look after the horse, Doctor," Dewey said firmly.

"All right, ma'am. Two days. But then we talk to Mrs. Downing. Ma'am." Still holding the syringe, the veterinarian went back to the stable, grabbed his bag, and then stalked off toward his car.

Dewey turned toward the stable. Peter Downing, his graceful form filling the doorway, seemed reluctant to let her pass. But offering neither apology nor explanation, Dewey squeezed past him and entered the building once more.

The little group within looked at her curiously.

"Hugh, I have made myself very bossy, I'm afraid."

"She saved him!" Willy cried in joyful tones. "Lady, did you save him?"

"Willy." Hugh's voice was firm. "This is 'Mrs. James' to you, son."

Dewey smiled. "Willy, you mustn't get your hopes up. We have thrown ourselves, however, on the mercy of the court, and found that it has a human heart, indeed. Hugh, Doctor Marvin has told me that I may take charge of Midnight for a few days. Only until Mrs. Downing is feeling well enough to be part of this decision. He is her property, after all, and rather valuable, too."

Peter Downing turned and, without a word, walked off toward the house. George, who had watched the entire transaction without speaking, now cocked an eyebrow at Dewey.

"I am not being sentimental, George. Hugh, can you arrange a trailer for us?"

The group leaped to action.

In less than an hour, with help from Hugh and Willy, Dewey had cleaned out the disused stall in Starbuck's small quarters. They had installed Midnight Blue there in comfortable, if temporary, security. Now Dewey, George, and Willy were sitting at her kitchen table, eating buttered toast with marmalade and drinking hot, sweet tea. Dewey proclaimed her old mare delighted to have the company. No one could say if Midnight understood how close a call he had had.

Willy's anxiety for Midnight had disappeared completely, although Dewey had gone to great pains to explain that this arrangement was only a momentary reprieve. So far were the boy's spirits recovered that he now recounted with gusto the discovery of the body. This glorious moment had been eclipsed, until now, by the shadow of death falling over Midnight Blue. Finally Willy had an audience.

"I was *petrified*," he asserted. "And you should have seen the horses. Were they ever spooked! When I put on the light, Midnight's ears were flat back against his head." He demonstrated with his hands.

"I think you did very well, Willy," said Dewey.

"Me, too," seconded George.

"And, I've never seen a dead body before. But now I have." Willy smoothed an even, careful layer of marmalade over his toast and cut the slice neatly in half before taking an enormous bite.

"Midnight never would have hurt Mr. Irish, though," Willy went on, looking puzzled. "I mean—he didn't really know Mr. Irish like he knows Hugh and me and the grooms. But he's incredibly gentle for a stallion."

"Well, I'm sure that something spooked him, that's all," said Dewey.

"But Midnight's not afraid of anything. Not anything. Except dead bodies, and who wouldn't be? He goes right past the tractors without pulling hard. We even rode by the skeet range one day and he didn't bolt."

"Amazing composure," said George, trying to sound informed.

"It's different at night," said Dewey. "When you wake the horses and it's dark, they can't see what's happening around them."

Midnight's predicament was apparent to them all once more. There was a brief, gloomy silence.

"Starbuck seems happy, anyway, to have company," said Dewey inanely. "The poor thing has been rather lonely in the last few years."

"Come on, Dewey," George expostulated.

"Now George—don't speak of what you know not of. Or something. In fact, the scientists will back me up."

"Oh?" asked George skeptically.

"Yes. There was a story published in *The New York Times* last year about some professors who spent fifteen years researching, in Vermont or somewhere."

"And what did they find out?"

"That horses like to be with other horses."

"No!" George laughed.

"That's *dumb*," said Willy. "Those people are professors?"

"Yes, and now they have empirical evidence of a sort that cannot be refuted. Which may, in the long run, be useful to some horse somewhere." George yawned. "But I agree, Willy. A little learning is a dangerous thing."

9

THE SERVICE FOR Donald Irish was scheduled for two o'clock on the Monday following the accident at Barnhouse. It was a cold, rainy day; the right kind of weather for a funeral, some might think. Dewey didn't think so. It had rained since before dawn, and by midmorning there was no sign that the downpour would let up. She shivered. She would not want to be laid to rest on such a cold, wet, unforgiving day.

In spite of the weather, Dewey was sure the service would be well attended; the good people of Hamilton would not let such an opportunity pass. To bear witness at the service would give them a chance to indulge their curiosity about Leslie Downing, whose degree of bereavement was a source of speculation; and about Peter, the prodigal son, mysteriously come home; and about Hugh Shields, the former favorite, the ex-right-hand-man. The event would be sure to feed the imagination of Hamilton.

"Rain, rain, go *away*!" Dewey muttered under her breath as she went to check on the horses. There had been so far no word from Barnhouse on Midnight Blue's fate; Leslie Downing had certainly been faced with more pressing matters, and Dewey was content not to stir the pot.

Willy had come every morning to help feed and water Midnight, but—much as the horse needed the exercise—Dewey couldn't allow the boy to take him out. Perhaps the veterinarian's death sentence would be forgotten somehow. Then Willy could ride.

It wasn't feeding time, but Dewey was drawn to the little

stable in her yard. Inside, where the air was warm and cozy, she perched atop the stall door and looked deeply into the stallion's eyes. The magnificent black horse nudged her; in his two days as Dewey's guest he had learned that there might be an apple or a carrot concealed in a pocket of her purple sweater.

"Nothing for you today, old fellow," said Dewey, stroking the smooth expanse of Midnight's cheek and running her hand down along his velvety neck. In two days she had grown to like Midnight rather a lot. What was more, she had realized something important. She was convinced the horse was not responsible for Irish's death. There was nothing of the killer in him.

Dewey roused herself from her reverie and gave Midnight a final pat. Then she went back indoors to phone George Farnham.

In his office at the Grain Merchant's Exchange, George was having a busy day. There was to be a hearing next week about rezoning farm properties for development, and the issue was, predictably, making everyone angry. This morning he had met with a formidable deputation from the Society for the Preservation of Hamilton Antiquities, whose members had spent forty-five minutes decrying the proposal. In vain George had tried to persuade them to save their arguments; his hands in the matter were tied, he explained. The proposal would be put to a council vote, and as president of the town council, George did not vote. He had finally managed to convince them that they would get a fair hearing in the matter, but the meeting had not been pleasant at all.

When Dewey phoned, therefore, George was in a snit.

"George, it's Dewey."

"Yes, Dewey."

"George, there is something I have to tell you. Can you meet me in half an hour for lunch?"

"Aren't you going to the funeral?"

"Yes, but—"

"Why don't we have a drink afterwards, then." George knew he sounded impatient. "I've had a terrible morning here, and I have to catch up a bit."

Dewey took a deep breath. "I think we have to talk before then. George, that man was killed!"

"Well of *course* he was killed. Near fore hoof to the temple, my dear. You're housing the felon, in case you've managed to forget."

"No, George, that's not what I mean. Please. It's important."

"All right, my dear. Josie's Place suit? Half an hour."

By the time she was comfortably ensconced in a booth at Josie's Place, waiting for George, Dewey had begun to doubt herself. It was one thing to feel, as you stroked a horse's nose, that you knew his character. It was quite another to admit to it in public. Here in the reasonable atmosphere of civilization, Dewey had to own that her conviction seemed fanciful. George would laugh at her—or worse, he would be polite.

George arrived, looking wet and cold, and sat down with a cordial smile. Dewey's heart sank. If only she had more to go on than this feeling!

She plunged right in. "You will probably tell me I'm crazy, I know, and half the town thinks I am, anyway. So you can join forces with them. And I probably am. Crazy."

"Dewey, calm down, calm down." George's reserve melted as Dewey's fond inanities washed over him in a wave. "Tell me what this important news is."

"Oh, George, I just know that horse is not a killer."

George was silent. She could tell that he was trying not to smile, which annoyed her.

"Don't go all supercilious on me, George Farnham."

"I promise to listen. But first, I need a little lunch." He picked up a menu and began to read it studiously. "Pea soup, I think, and a grilled cheese for me. What will you have, my dear?"

"The same. Now—"

"One second. 'Arf a tick, as the English say." He looked around for the waitress.

"You're not listening, George."

"That's because you haven't said anything yet, my friend." A young waitress arrived to take their order. That transaction completed, George settled in to listen.

"Okay. Shoot."

"I have been thinking about this long and hard. I need you to hear me out. Now. Being a man-about-town, you probably don't realize that horses have characters, just as we do."

"I cannot claim to have conversed with Mister Ed, but I have read my Anna Sewell, at least," quipped George.

"I'm serious. When an animal—any animal, not necessarily a horse—is mean enough to kill, that meanness shows. When it has killed once, it will do so again. The meanness peeps through even the most thorough of training. Love and murder will out. That's why Doctor Marvin was ready to put Midnight down."

"It's psychological," said George.

"That's right. And I am quite sure Midnight didn't do this deed."

"Dewey, dear, I think it's noble of you to want to save the horse from a premature demise. Begging your pardon, however, I do not see the urgency of the issue. Has someone tried to remove the horse from your tender care?"

"You're missing the point, George. You see—" Dewey broke off hastily as their lunches were brought "—the horse is just a scapegoat. So to speak. But—" she picked up her soup spoon and waved it at George "—if Midnight didn't kill Irish by accident, then someone else must have. By design." She gave him a look and dipped into her soup.

George gazed carefully at his friend. He knew Dewey too well—loved her too well—to go along with the conventional town wisdom that she was dotty. Her fey air was amusing, but George suspected that it was a smoke screen. For insecurity, perhaps; or perhaps for a deadly seriousness about life. He did not doubt her intelligence. Dewey was not always logical, but she was often right. He examined the proposition she had set before him as Dewey ate her soup in silence.

"Do we have anything to go on," George asked at last, "other than your examination of the defendant's character?"

"Don't be flip. There must be something. I have the feeling that I know something concrete. For starters, if Midnight was spooked, I don't believe the mere presence of Donald Irish in the stable would do it. A loud noise, perhaps, I grant you. Or being struck with a whip suddenly. But Willy found the body. Did he or Hugh or any of the others mention that they found something that could have startled the horse?"

"Not that I recall."

"If Irish had used a whip, someone would have found it; Willy would have seen it. He has a real eye for detail, that boy."

"Hmmm."

"He does. Plus, the race was going to be his big day. He would have noticed. But if there was *someone else* present, the goad—whatever it was—would have been removed."

"I take your point."

"Well, then! If there was somebody else there, why hasn't the person come forward? George, the man was murdered."

"Dewey, let's not get ahead of ourselves. We'll think this one through carefully. Now, let's try to recall everything Willy told us about finding the body."

They went over the boy's story step by step. On Saturday morning, after bringing Midnight to Dewey's house, Willy had supplied a vivid account of the pandemonium in the stables: the naked terror that had overcome the horses in the presence of the dead man, the urgency with which the men at Barnhouse had responded to Willy's summons for help.

"Doctor Marvin says there was a blow to the temple, and bloodstains on Midnight's hoof," said Dewey.

"So you told me," responded George. "Near fore."

"But let's see." Dewey drew a stout fountain pen from her handbag and hastily began to sketch Midnight's stall on the paper place mat. "Here is Midnight." She drew a square, then two ears above a long nose protruding over its edges. "And Irish was *here*." A rough outline of a body, delineated in the best tradition of forensic chalk markings, appeared on the mat. "The door to the stall is here, on the left—" she made two little marks "on what would be the *right* side of the horse."

"Surely the horse might have turned around."

"There is room enough, perhaps. We would have to measure the box," Dewey conceded. "But I doubt he did. Every time I go to call on Midnight he puts his head right out over the little wall. He likes to face his visitors."

"Dewey."

"He *does*, George. Now. If Irish walked into that stall, and spooked Midnight so badly that the horse struck him—and remember, if you please, what Willy said about the horse's calmness at the skeet range—the bloodstains would be on the other hoof. Or at least, there would be bloodstains on both." Dewey drew a rudimentary horse and circled both forelegs.

George sat back in the booth, impressed by her reasoning, if not by her drafting skill.

"Dewey, you may be on to something."

"I think we should see the police. Let's go right away, George. There may be a killer on the loose."

"I have a better idea," said George. "If Irish was murdered, then our killer probably thinks he's safe. You can bet that if the police had been questioning anyone, we would have heard about it lickety-split. I think that before we raise the alarm, we ought to attend the poor man's funeral."

Dewey shot George an appreciative, conspiratorial look. "Yes. In our customary suits of solemn black." She tugged her purple sweater on and stood up. "Shall we?"

10

THE CHURCH OF the Good Shepherd, like the Grain Merchants' Exchange where George Farnham now had his office, had been built in times of greater prosperity in Hamilton. It was a large brick structure, beautifully proportioned, with a perfect steeple at the top. The carillon, once grand but now sadly out of tune, was giving out a mournful approximation of "Abide with Me" as Dewey and George made their hurried way through the downpour into the building.

As Dewey had predicted, and in spite of the foul weather, poor Donald Irish had attracted a respectable turnout on this, his big day. Dewey looked at the crowd and thought about the soul-searching she had done on Thursday as she drove home from Jensen's Feed & Grain. It was pitiful that a man so apparently friendless in life should be suddenly popular on his leaving it. It was worse to think that someone had wanted so pitiful a fellow to die.

The entire staff of the Warren State Savings and Loan had turned out to say farewell to their late colleague, as had most of the merchants in town. Dewey supposed that many of these people had been, albeit briefly, Irish's clients. At least they had known him. What excuse did Dewey have for turning up, other than ghoulish curiosity?

As they found seats toward the back of the church, George seemed to read her discomfort. He gave her a serious look and nodded across the aisle. Fielding Booker, captain of the Hamilton police force, was in attendance. George raised an eyebrow at Dewey.

"Oh, my," said Dewey, turning to the printed program and giving it all her attention. Hymns, psalms, eulogy. The interment would be private, she read.

As the organ sounded the first notes of "Oh, God Our Help In Ages Past," Dewey ventured another look around at the congregation. There was a sizable contingent from Barnhouse. Leslie Downing was there, elegant in a beautiful suit of deep charcoal gray; seated behind her were several of the stable hands. A serious-looking Willy Grimes, with a necktie round his throat, sat beside a pretty, redheaded woman of about forty; no doubt his mother, Dewey reflected. Hugh Shields was alone in the last pew, leaning forward in a devotional attitude. There was no sign of Peter Downing.

Dewey roused herself from this macabre inventory to join in the Twenty-third Psalm. This was followed by the minister's eulogy—brief and discouragingly polite.

When the service was concluded, Dewey and George caught up with Fielding Booker on the church steps. Booker had been second-in-command of the tiny police force in the days when Dewey's husband, Brendan, had been captain. Early in his career, Booker had broken up a notorious gambling ring that had been putting the muscle on stable owners in the area. Ever since, he had been known to one and all, inevitably, as "Bookie." Dewey counted him an old friend.

"Bookie, how are you?" she asked in hushed tones.

"Hello, Dewey. Well, thank you. Afternoon, George." Booker was tall and strongly built, about fifty-five, and very handsome. His thick black hair was only now beginning to turn gray, matching his attention-getting eyebrows. He was a stylish man, proud of his good looks, and he had always spurned the police uniform in favor of old-fashioned but extremely well-cut suits. Today he sported a silk, double-breasted suit of a superior cut. The look was pure Sam Spade.

In the old days, Dewey and Brendan had joked about Bookie's incongruous elegance. Brendan James had been a rough-and-ready type, a cop's cop. Bookie, his right-hand man, was something else again.

Dewey's husband had told her that Booker had once dreamed of a greatness beyond the parochial confines of

Hamilton. He had longed to be a Scotland Yard inspector, or the mastermind behind an exclusive detective agency. Unfortunately, Fielding Booker was no Sherlock Holmes. Behind that imposing brow, beneath that elegant veneer, there lurked the intellect and intuition of a mere Watson.

Luckily for Hamiltonians, their resident sleuth was rarely called upon to detect anything. The quiet little town offered slim pickings for detectives, even for so stylish and willing an investigator. Dewey secretly suspected that, should Booker's talents really be put to the test, a touch of the Clouseau would emerge.

"Well, well. Dewey, George. What brings you two out on this miserable day? Knew the fellow, did you?"

"Yes, er, we ah—" began Dewey.

"It is a rotten day, no question," put in George, looking out at the sheeting rain. "What say we all pop around to my place for some hot tea, or something a little stronger?"

Booker consulted his gold pocket watch. "Not much doing today. I think I can leave the safety of our little community in my subordinates' hands for a few hours."

The three set off for George Farnham's house.

Farnham lived about half a mile from the church. His children were a long time grown and gone, and at his wife's death he had sold their big frame house and purchased a small, old mill in the center of town, overlooking the river. Many Hamiltonians had thereupon concluded that grief had left George imbalanced; but in five years he had single-handedly transformed the empty factory into a beautiful home.

The three sat in the kitchen around a spacious, clean-lined oak table while the kettle warmed on an enormous, industrial-looking stove. Sliding glass doors led to a riverside terrace, and they watched as, outside, the rain whipped down in sheets. While they waited for the kettle to boil, Dewey talked gamely about the changes at the library. She wasn't quite sure how to begin, now that she had Booker's attention.

"All right, now, you two," said Booker finally, accepting a cup of tea. "Enough about the library, Dewey. Let's have it. I sense that there is something up here."

Dewey took a deep breath. "Bookie, she said, "before you tell me I'm loony, I think you should hear me out."

Booker smiled. He had a great deal of affection for his late captain's widow, but she was definitely around the bend. He had heard, through the fail-safe Hamilton grapevine, that she had taken Midnight Blue under her eccentric wing. He had an idea of what was coming.

"Yes, Dewey?"

"Bookie, have you looked carefully into Donald Irish's death?"

The question obviously surprised him. "I'm not sure I know just what you mean, Dewey. Charlie O'Donovan examined him, you know. The coroner was satisfied. Listen, Dewey, if this is about that horse—"

"Well, it is, and it isn't. Bookie, I think you should look into the facts of the case more closely."

"The case? Dewey—" Bookie sighed. He looked into his teacup, stirring its contents thoughtfully. "Dewey, we can't save that horse. Not if he killed a man. I'm very sorry."

"But what if he didn't?"

"I don't follow you."

"Bookie, I think—that is, I've explained it to George, and he thought I should talk to you. I think Donald Irish was murdered."

"Now, Dewey."

"Just hear me out, Bookie. You promised you would."

Booker had made no such promise, but he was willing enough to listen. Dewey began to tell him about her reading of the horse's character. Booker threw George a glance.

"Let's put all that aside for now, Dewey, dear," broke in George, "and show Bookie your reconstruction of the scene."

"Oh, yes, good thinking, George." Dewey reached for her handbag and produced from within its fastness a folded and stained paper place mat. "Look at this, Booker. I drew this for George earlier when he didn't believe me."

Carefully she led the police captain through the elements of her argument, using her lunchtime drawings as visual aids. When she was done, Booker sat back in his chair. He looked from Dewey to George and back again.

"By God," he said.

"Then you agree with me," said Dewey soberly.

"I think it's worth an investigation." Booker looked concerned. "I'll have to speak to the coroner. He'll be able to shed a little light on the manner of death." He ran his hands through his hair. "I wish we had thought about this earlier. I didn't even go out there on Saturday. The whole thing was so straightforward."

"Will you have to get an exhumation order?" asked George.

"No, we're lucky there." Booker shifted in his chair and looked disconsolately at his tea. "Do you have a little something stronger, George?"

"Bourbon do for you?"

"Perfect." George rose and went to the liquor cabinet. "We're lucky there," Booker repeated. He might have been referring to the bourbon.

He leaned back in his chair, hands behind his head, and stared up at the ceiling. "It seems this man Irish has a family plot somewhere near Chicago. Hodgkins is sending the body there for burial. They couldn't arrange transport until tomorrow, though. He's still at the funeral home."

George put a drink before the policeman. Booker stirred the ice cubes distractedly with his finger, but did not pick up the glass.

"What put you on to this idea, Dewey?" he asked at last.

"The horse."

"I see." Booker tried to sound sincere.

"You see, Bookie, that stallion is no more a killer than I am. You can tell these things about animals."

"Is that so." He sipped at his drink. "Well, to each his own." Booker looked at George inquiringly.

"We also had a long chat with that young stableboy, Willy," added George.

"I know he's just a child, Bookie," put in Dewey earnestly, "but he is quite an organized young man. You should see how he cares for the equipment at Barnhouse."

"Have you been talking to people at Barnhouse?" Booker looked annoyed. Dewey blushed.

"Not about Irish's death," George reassured him quickly. He seemed a bit embarrassed himself.

"Last week, before the—all this," said Dewey. "We—I was curious about the race. So I thought I'd pay a call on Leslie Downing. I just wondered if I could find out what was going on at Barnhouse."

"Like everybody else in town," agreed Booker. He took a pull at his glass and stood up. "I'm off. I suppose, Dewey, I ought to thank you. I'll let you know if this idea of yours is—if anything turns up. George." He bowed slightly and took up his umbrella and hat. Farnham rose and saw him to the door.

"Well, Dewey, my dear," said George, returning. "I think you made your case. Feeling better?"

Dewey looked unhappily at her friend. " 'There shall be done a deed of dreadful note.' " She crossed her arms on the table and put her head down. "Better? Lord, no, George. This is awful."

11

HAVING SET JUSTICE in motion in the person of Fielding Booker, Dewey tried to fix her mind on something else—on anything that would distract her from the specter of that violent death in Midnight Blue's stall. When she arrived home on Monday evening, therefore, she called Tom Campbell, the new librarian, to schedule a meeting for the Literacy Volunteers Committee for the following day.

Nonetheless, as she sat down at her kitchen table to work out some details of the project, she found her mind straying once more to that scene. She grimly imagined Irish groping his way in the darkened stable, letting himself into Midnight's stall—but why? What on earth had brought him there in the night?

Irish clearly spent a great deal of time at Barnhouse, exercising his talents in a variety of subjects. But he was a financial type, not a riding man. His main interest was business, even if his interest in Leslie Downing was something else again. Why would he go to the stables at night?

Dewey recalled the scene at Jensen's Feed & Grain: Irish complaining to Rob Jensen. Had he been talking about the feed? Or the price? More likely, it was the price. Dewey tried to remember. No, it had been the feed. Odd.

He went to the stable at night to check on something, then. Or to meet with someone, quietly. He could have been trying to get to the bottom of something that had puzzled him. Something wrong at Barnhouse.

Dewey frowned. What about the new man, the new trainer

57

who had been brought in? Mark Gordon. Why had Leslie Downing hired a new trainer just now? Was it Irish's idea?

Two newcomers to Hamilton, and it seemed both were part of the disruption of a revered Hamilton tradition. Was there a connection?

Even if Leslie Downing had not wanted Hugh to ride in the point-to-point, there were plenty of able bodies around for that kind of job. Bodies.

Dewey shivered and reached down automatically to scratch Isaiah, who was, as usual, asleep at her feet. "Good old boy, good old Isaiah," she said softly. He opened one eye and looked at her. Dewey got up and peered out the kitchen window. The rain had stopped, at long last, but the ground was soaked. Maybe it was too wet for Isaiah to sleep in his doghouse tonight.

Perhaps, Dewey admitted to herself, she would feel safer with him in the house. She whistled to her dog, put out the light, and the two of them headed upstairs.

Tuesday was a beautiful spring day, warm and breezy. Dewey rose early and went out to see to the horses. Her anxiety of the previous night was gone, leaving behind a fierce curiosity. The situation was unbearable—murder at Barnhouse! As she headed outdoors, Willy Grimes came pedaling up the driveway on his bike.

"Good morning, Willy," Dewey called, trying to sound cheery.

"Hi, Mrs. James," said Willy. "Have you heard anything yet?" He dismounted and leaned his bike up against the little stable. For a second, Dewey thought the boy was referring to the murder. She gave him a strange look.

"About Midnight, Mrs. James. Has Mrs. Downing said anything?"

"No, dear, not yet. But you mustn't get your hopes up too high. In spite of what they say about no news." She opened the door to the stable.

The horses looked up as Dewey and Willy entered. Midnight proffered his nose for stroking as Willy approached. "He's really a good horse, Mrs. James. I don't think he meant any harm."

"Indeed he is," concurred Dewey. She watched Willy as he moved confidently about Midnight's stall, cleaning it, pouring in fresh water, bringing fresh oats. There was no fear in the boy at all. Her instincts had been right. This horse was not a killer.

"Hey, Mrs. James, I have an idea."

"What's that, Willy?"

"Well, maybe if Midnight doesn't have to die, and you don't want him, maybe Mrs. Downing would sell him to me."

"I think he would come very expensive, Willy."

"Yeah, but I've got it all worked out. I could own him, and look after him, and Mrs. Downing could ride him whenever she wanted. Or lease him out for stud, and she would still get the fee. This way she could have more room."

"Does she need more room?" asked Dewey, spilling a small cascade of oats into Starbuck's trough.

"There are four mares in foal at Barnhouse. That's a lot of stalls they'll need, and Hugh was saying that he told Mr. Irish that they should build a new stable block. Only Mr. Irish thought it would be too expensive. And if they sold the foals when they were yearlings, new stables would be like money down the drain."

He scattered some fresh hay about the floor. "Loaning Midnight to me would be kind of like a business deal," he finished up in a professional tone.

"Indeed," said Dewey. "It would be exactly like a business deal. I congratulate you on your astute grasp of the opportunities."

Willy grinned. "You think it might work?"

"If things go well for Midnight," said Dewey, looking sadly at the stallion. Midnight's huge nostrils flared, and he gave a loud snort.

They had finished in the stable. "How about some lingonberry bread, Willy?" said Dewey cordially.

"What's that?"

"Kind of like blueberry muffins. Only made with something that's more like cranberries."

"Great!" They ambled back to the house, where Dewey

made a pot of hot chocolate for Willy and coffee for herself as she tried to think of an opening. There were some questions she needed to ask, but her interlocutor, she recognized, was very shrewd. If she wasn't careful, he might know something strange was afoot.

"Willy," she said when they were seated over their breakfast, "I'm very glad to have your help with Midnight. But doesn't Hugh need you at Barnhouse in the mornings?"

"Yeah. Well, he told me to take a few days off. *With* pay. Because of the accident." Willy took a huge bite of his lingonberry bread.

"That was kind of him."

"He's a nice guy. Besides, there's not much going on right now."

"Even with a new trainer to be broken in?"

"Nah. He knows his way around. He's leaving tomorrow, anyway, for a race in Maryland. Stanley Steamer. *What* a horse that is, Mrs. James."

"Is he?" Dewey stirred her coffee distractedly, feeling at a loss. How could she get to the bottom of this, without alarming Willy?

She needn't have worried. It was Willy's turn to alarm her.

"You know what, Mrs. James?" he asked, reaching for another slice of bread. "There's something I've been wondering about."

"What's that?"

"How come Mr. Irish didn't turn on the light in the stable?"

"What do you mean, Willy?" She felt a prickle of fear. This was something she hadn't even considered. Starbuck's stable had no electricity.

"Say you went to check on Starbuck. You don't have a light switch, I noticed that. But if you did, and if you went out there in the night, wouldn't you turn on the light?"

"Yes, I suppose I would, Willy." Dewey concurred.

"See, if Mr. Irish had turned on the light, then Midnight would have seen him and not been spooked. Then everything would be fine." Willy's eyes began to fill with tears. "It wasn't Midnight's fault if someone snuck up on him in the dark, was it? I think we should tell Doctor Marvin. Will you tell Doctor Marvin?"

Dewey took a deep breath. "Willy, I think you have raised a very good point in Midnight's defense. More hot chocolate?"

Tom Campbell, the new librarian, had a captive audience in the Literacy Volunteers Committee. The little group was assembled in the crowded staff room behind the librarian's office. The place doubled as a storage area for books in need of repair, shipping documents, and files, so meetings always had an informal look.

Today there were five people crammed in the tiny room. Dewey and Susan Miles occupied the only chairs in the place; everyone else sat on upturned crates or small file cabinets. Tom Campbell took full advantage, droning on, and on, and on.

"And so, my feeling is that we ought bravely to eschew the expenditure of the library's meager resources for the tutoring program. We must put ourselves fully behind a program whose stated purpose is the safeguarding of our collection. I agree with the members of this committee that the installation of security devices will prove expensive. I venture to suggest that the watchful maintenance of our current assets is, and must needs be, our primary responsibility. May I take it that we are all in agreement on this point?"

He finished up in rounded tones, drawing himself up to his full five feet seven inches. He gazed around at the small group before him, looking on them with diffident pride as he concluded his lengthy exhortation. His cheeks had a proud flush, and his small chest was puffed out. He was trying not to look in Dewey's direction as he cast about for support of his heretical policy. He needn't have worried about her opposition, however; Dewey had bigger fish to fry. She was lost in thought.

"No, you may not, Mr. Campbell." Dewey looked with surprise at the speaker. It was Nils Reichart, proprietor of the Seven Locks Tavern, a local bar and pool hall. Dewey had been pleased, if surprised, when he had joined the committee; for he was not known as a great reader, and rarely used the library.

"Mr. Campbell, you will probably not call me an intellectual type." Campbell smiled wanly. The librarian's idea of who did qualify as an intellectual in Hamilton was clearly limited to a quorum of one. Reichart went on. "But I do some rehab work with inmates over at the Calvert prison. Some of them never even finished grade school. We have to help them, teach them to read. No way can they get along, make a new life, if they can't read. No way."

"Surely, Mr. Reichart," said Campbell archly, "the scenario you have just conjured for us would be calculated to leave the library somewhat more exposed than before." He pronounced the word "lie-bree."

"Tom, really!" said Susan Miles acidly.

Campbell's face showed an irritable complacency. "I merely put the point to the committee," he said blandly, "that we are now experiencing an epidemic of theft in the library. We are surely not going to be aided in our attempts to stem the—the outflow, if you will, by inviting convicted felons into our midst."

Dewey's abstracted mood was departing. This man really got under her skin.

"Ahem." Dewey cleared her throat. Campbell looked at her. "If I might make a suggestion?" she said, in her most innocent tones.

Oh boy, thought Susan Miles, we're in for something now.

"Yes, Mrs. James."

"Oh, Tom, do stop with the formality. Please. Call me Dewey. We *are* colleagues." She smiled. Campbell sat down moodily on a file cabinet.

"Well, then." Dewey smiled at the group. "If you will bear with me while I think out loud. Mr. Reichart has set me thinking. His speech has prompted a most interesting association of ideas. The Mikado."

Susan Miles coughed gently. Dewey continued. "You remember that the Mikado wished to condemn the pool sharp—not *you*, Mr. Reichart, don't misunderstand me!—to play on 'a cloth untrue, with a twisted cue, and elliptical billard balls.' Now, if I were to take up a hobby—such as skydiving, for example—"

There was a spasm of stifled laughter in the little room. Dewey looked around innocently.

"—I would not ask for instruction from the people who send up hot air balloons. If you follow me."

Nobody, of course, did. Dewey plunged ahead. "We have two things at work here, but I see how they could be made one. So to speak. What if we were to sponsor a program in reading for some of Mr. Reichart's prison inmates?"

"Ah—" began Campbell.

"One minute, Tom," said Dewey sweetly, fixing him with a look. "In turn, we could ask them to take part in a new security program. Because if anyone knows how theft is best accomplished, it is they."

"Mrs.—Dewey, isn't that rather a 'fox at the henhouse' style of thing?" asked Campbell.

"Honestly, Tom, I doubt they were sent up the river for stealing novels," put in Susan Miles. Reichart laughed. "I think it's a good idea, Dewey."

"Me, too," said Reichart. "We could figure out an exchange—like trading an afternoon of tutoring for an afternoon of work as a security guard. Calvert has a lot of inmates on a kind of limited work-release thing. They drop them off at their jobs and pick them up. The guys just have to wear one of those radio ankle-bracelet jobs. It could work out real well."

"Splendid," said Henry List, the drama teacher from Hamilton High, who had not spoken thus far. "Terrific. Those guys will certainly intimidate the less hardened criminals in our midst. They can steal about on catlike tread, and all that. Keep an eye on things." He smiled at Dewey. "Let's put it to a vote. All in favor?"

"Aye." Four voices.

"Opposed?"

Tom Campbell fumed silently.

"Done." List turned to Reichart. "Why don't you talk to the prison officials and see what we can work out?"

"Will do. Thanks, Mrs. James," Reichart said to Dewey.

"Please call me Dewey. It is I who should thank you."

The meeting broke up.

* * *

"Nice work, Dewey," said Susan Miles. The two women stood on the library steps.

"I feel badly about that," responded Dewey. But the cheerful look on her face belied the statement.

"You mean you would like to feel bad," corrected Susan. "If the man weren't such a twit—"

"Shh!" urged Dewey with a look around. "He'll learn, I hope," she went on. They descended the small flight of granite steps and headed together up Main Street. "He's so solemn that it's comical. Like Pooh-bah, the Lord High Everything Else. But he'll relax. He's still quite young."

"Tom Campbell was never young. He was born old."

Dewey began to laugh as she envisioned a tiny Tom Campbell in snap shirt and diapers, removing a pacifier from his mouth to make speeches to his mother. "Just imagine him as a baby, Susan," Dewey chuckled, "repudiating his pablum. 'I don't care for strained carrots, Mother, if you take my meaning,' " she mimicked.

Giggling, they arrived at Susan's car. "Can I give you a lift?"

"Oh, no thanks, dear. I think I may pop around to call on George at his office."

"Hmmm," said Susan meaningfully. She opened the car door and climbed in.

"Oh, Susan, don't be daft." Dewey looked uncomfortable.

"I didn't say a word, Dewey. Not a word." She smiled. "About how you and George don't let a day go by . . ."

"Don't tease me, Susan." Dewey was perfectly willing to let the seeds of gossip sprout, for once. Rumors of romance, no matter how unsubstantiated, were far preferable to rumors of murder.

Susan Miles drove away. Taking a deep breath, Dewey retraced her steps past the library and turned in at a small brick building on the corner. The lettering on the door read HAMILTON POLICE. Dewey had something important to tell Fielding Booker.

12

DEWEY HADN'T ENTERED the Hamilton police headquarters since Brendan's death, six years ago, and she was unprepared for the emotions that overwhelmed her now. Everything looked exactly the same. The radiator to the left of the door was draped familiarly with a varied array of hats and coats—they still hadn't got 'round to putting in a proper closet, thought Dewey. The walls, made of thin panels of oak, were scarred and pitted. Straight ahead, a narrow corridor led to a series of small offices. On the right was a countertop that held wire baskets of paper, a calendar, a telephone, and a huge, black rotating fan. It hummed busily, kicking up papers on the counter as it made its little journey: all the way left, pause, then all the way right. Even in winter that fan stayed on. The back of the building held a tiny cell block, and ventilation was always poor.

The place smelled the same, too, giving off a mixture of bad coffee, pipe tobacco, and the standard, office-issue aroma that marks institutions around the globe. Brendan had brought a raggedy whiff of this scent with him when he came home at night. Suddenly, Dewey missed him terribly.

"Afternoon, Mrs. James," said a cheery voice. Dewey started. A young man in uniform was advancing down the narrow corridor toward her.

"Oh—it's—"

"Fenton, ma'am. Mike Fenton."

"Yes, Officer Fenton."

"Sergeant, ma'am," the policeman said politely.

"Well, young man, I congratulate you. Indeed I do." Dewey

65

was getting her bearings again. She had not known this would be so hard. "How is Ellen?"

"Good, good. We're expecting our second next month."

"How lovely."

"Anything I can help you with today, ma'am?"

"I wondered if I might have a word with Captain Booker."

"Sure thing. I'll tell him you're here." He looked at Dewey with curiosity before retreating down the corridor. She wondered briefly if her suspicions had been made known to the force. There was a sudden knot in her stomach. Her idea was crazy. They had undoubtedly spent the morning laughing at her. Dewey James must have a slate loose. Always thought she was too fond of horses. Have you heard the latest? Hah-hah. Hah-hah.

"Dewey, come on in." Fielding Booker had stolen up on her. Today he wore a beautiful Depression-era pinstripe straight out of *The Untouchables*.

"Oh, Bookie, I don't want to bother you."

"No, bother, no bother. I tried to reach you earlier, but there was no answer." He led her down the hall to his office and made her comfortable in an old wooden armchair facing his desk.

"I'd offer you coffee, but I don't relish a charge of attempted poisoning." He sat down in the chair behind the desk. Dewey's mouth was dry.

"This must be kind of hard for you, isn't it, Dewey?" Booker was leaning forward, looking intently at his guest. "I'll bet you haven't been in this office since Brendan . . ."

"That's right." Dewey took hold of herself. "I wasn't expecting it to be so much the same."

"We all miss him, you know. I think about him every day. And I still think of this as his office. Can't help myself."

"Bookie, you're so kind." Dewey was feeling better. But what a day it had been!

"Now. Down to business."

"Oh, Bookie, what have you found out? Tell me I'm crazy. Go ahead."

"You may be crazy, Dewey," said Booker with a laugh, "but damned if you weren't right." He was suddenly quite serious. "The M.E. from the coroner's office has had another look at that wound." He stabbed at a sheaf of computer print-out paper on his desk. "It was difficult because of the mortician's preparations. We might have missed it. But the medical examiner found some microscopic traces of particulate matter in the wound that aren't consistent with the presumed blow from the horse."

"I knew it." Dewey sat up. "Murder."

"Now, Dewey, I don't want you jumping to conclusions. Leave it to the police."

"Of course, Bookie, of course," Dewey replied in abstracted tones. "I wonder why Charlie O'Donovan missed it."

"He wasn't looking for it."

"Naturally not," said Dewey. "Well. What's our next step, Bookie?"

Booker looked at her uncomfortably. "Dewey, I appreciate your interest. And I thank you for your suggestions. But from now on, it's a police matter. I can't discuss it."

"That's fair enough," said Dewey, looking utterly unconvinced. "Just tell me—have you talked to Leslie about it?"

"I saw her this morning, but I haven't mentioned my suspicions. We discussed the paper work for the county health department. In the event that the horse is put down." He looked at Dewey sternly. "You're not to breathe a word about the matter, Dewey."

"Of course, Bookie. Rely on me."

Booker rose. "Reply on *us,* Dewey. I don't want you wondering and worrying about things." He came around the desk. The interview was clearly at an end.

"If I could make one tiny suggestion, Bookie?" asked Dewey, rising.

Booker looked at her patiently. "Yes?"

"I think you should speak to Willy."

"Who?"

"The stableboy, Willy Grimes. He told me and George on Saturday that he had been at Barnhouse Friday night, polishing Midnight's bridle."

Booker leaned across his desk and made a note. "What time did he leave?"

"I couldn't say. But I'm sure it wasn't late. Saturday was to be his big day, handling the horse for the point-to-point. He is an independent soul, but he does have a mother."

"Don't we all. Well, Dewey, thank you very much. Again." Booker was ready to return to work. The discussion was at an end. It was just as well, thought Dewey, as she gathered up her handbag. The whole thing made her sick at heart. But what if Booker missed another important point? After all, it had been Dewey herself who started the investigation.

"There is just one other thing, Bookie," said Dewey, as he walked her down the corridor.

"What's that?"

"Willy mentioned it to me, you see, this morning over his breakfast."

"Dewey, you haven't told that boy—"

"Really, Bookie. Of course not. Don't be silly."

"All right, Dewey. Sorry. What is it?"

"The lights. In the stable. They were off when he got there at five-thirty on Saturday morning. That, I think, is something you should know."

"Yes, well, thanks, Dewey." Booker had begun to look impatient.

"I don't have electricity in Starbuck's little stable, of course, so I didn't think about that. But Willy quite rightly pointed out that Irish would have turned on the lights. If he had gone there on his own. Because, you see, he didn't know his way around a stable in the dark. Unless you found a flashlight at the scene."

"I see." Booker was noncommittal. Dewey wondered if he had thought to look for a flashlight.

Booker changed the topic. "Dewey, I'm sure I don't have to tell you that all of this must be strictly between us. And George, of course." He opened the front door of the office for her. "If I'm right about this business, we may be up against someone quite dangerous. I don't want to have to worry about you."

"Have no fear, Bookie. I shall be quiet as the grave."

She took her leave.

13

IT MAY WELL be imagined that, in spite of Dewey's promise to keep silent about her suspicions, the visit of Captain Booker to Barnhouse had prompted uneasiness and speculation. Leslie Downing, in her time, had seen a good many horses put down. Never had the occasion necessitated a visit from the captain of the police. It was just as well for all concerned, then, that the news was soon made official.

By lunchtime on Wednesday, the day after Dewey's visit to him, Captain Booker had received further findings from the county medical examiner's office. Shorn of its medico-legal mumbo-jumbo, the report indicated that Donald Irish had actually perished as a result of asphyxiation. The time of death was put at between ten and midnight, give or take. The blow to the head, it was determined, had been a mighty one, and could easily have proved fatal in time. But the man had been suffocated, as well. This fact accounted for the victim's limited loss of blood; for the engine of life had ceased its cheery hum shortly after the wallop was administered.

At about five o'clock, therefore, Captain Booker made his way up the long drive to Barnhouse in the company of Sergeant Mike Fenton.

"Why don't you look around, Mike, while I talk to the lady of the house?" Booker said as he made his way to the front door.

Leslie Downing answered the door herself.

"Good afternoon, Mrs. Downing," said Booker politely. The mistress of Barnhouse looked surprised to see him.

"Back again, Captain?" She wore beautifully cut green woolen trousers and an expensive-looking black turtleneck under a heavy, hand-knit sweater of gold and brown. Her short black hair, neatly cut, swung gracefully out from behind her ears. She gave Booker a tentative smile and opened the door wide. "Come on in." She stepped back smoothly a step or two, allowing Booker to pass. "I was just going to have a cocktail. Will you join me?" She led the way toward the living room.

"No, thank you, ma'am." Booker followed. "I think perhaps you'd better sit down."

"I appreciate your concern, Captain," Leslie smiled, "but one gets used to these things. Midnight Blue is not the first horse we have had to put down at Barnhouse." She sat anyway, in a deep, round-backed armchair made of rosewood, with plum-colored upholstery on the seat and arms. She gestured to the sofa opposite. Booker took a seat.

"I'm afraid I have some bad news, Mrs. Downing," he began, sounding a little self-important. "I've just had a report from the county medical examiner. It appears that Mr. Irish's death was a little complicated." He regarded her with concern. "Too complicated, in fact, to be the result of being kicked by a horse."

Leslie's brow furrowed. "What are you saying, Captain?"

"We have reason to believe that he was murdered, Mrs. Downing."

Leslie Downing went pale and stiffened momentarily in her chair. Then she looked straight at Booker, her steady gray eyes focused clearly on his.

"I think you had better tell me all about it, Captain," she said. The tremor in her voice belied her composure. "Sure you won't join me in a drink?"

"No, thank you."

She stood up abruptly and crossed the room to a small mahogany tray table that held a silver ice bucket. Beside the ice bucket were half a dozen matching glasses, ornate with hand-painted grouse. Three decanters stood in a row, with silver labels hanging around their necks.

Booker waited as Leslie Downing reached for a decanter that was half-full of something clear and poured a stiff shot.

"Captain?" She walked back to the chair and sat down again, crossing elegant legs.

"Mr. Irish died as a result of asphyxiation—cutting off of oxygen to the brain."

"I see. Couldn't that have taken place as a result of—of the blow, or falling down in the stable?"

"I'm afraid not, ma'am. Not according to the medical report. No need to go into detail. But I'm afraid this means, of course, that we shall have to spend quite a bit of time here, examining the scene, and so forth. And we will have to ask for statements from everyone who was present here on Friday night. Yourself included."

"Of course, Captain. Anything I can do to help. Or my staff."

"Thank you. You'll make this all a great deal easier for us."

"Not at all. Is there anything that I can do right now?"

"Actually, yes. Perhaps you would come with me to the stable where the incident occurred. My sergeant is there now, but I think maybe we could use your help. We're neither of us horse people."

"Let's go, then." She stood.

The stable where Irish had been found dead lay about three hundred yards from the house. Fielding Booker followed Leslie Downing through a little grove of fir trees, across a small field, and down a hill. Here the land spread out before them, broken only by undulating lines of white fencing that marked the boundaries of the big pastures beyond. Farther still, behind the pasture, was a line of trees. A large sky pond far off on the left shimmered in the late afternoon sun; in the distance, a half-dozen figures of deep chestnut and bay moved lazily about. The scene was remarkably peaceful and beautiful. As they walked, Leslie Downing told Booker a little bit about the way Barnhouse was run. On the night of Irish's death, she explained, there had been only a handful of staff about the place—one or two stable hands, the new trainer, and Hugh Shields.

"As well as your son Peter."

"That's right, Captain." Leslie Downing walked with long,

even strides, surefooted on the familiar terrain. Booker was a tall man, but he had to move briskly to keep up with her.

"Mrs. Downing," said Booker, "I'm sure you'll understand that I must ask a great many awkward questions at times like these."

"So I would imagine."

"Well then. Suppose I get one of these off my chest, right away."

"I imagine you'd like to ask me about my relationship to Donald."

"That's it exactly."

"So—ask away, Captain."

"It had reached my ears, ma'am, that there was something in the nature of romance between the two of you."

"You're in the right ball park, Captain."

"I see. Forgive me for asking, ma'am—but was there a business relationship between you, as well?"

Leslie Downing chuckled heartily and threw Booker an appreciative glance. "That's the first amusing thing anyone has said to me in weeks, Captain." She chuckled again.

"It wasn't all that funny," Booker said.

"Better than nothing." She seemed to have unbent considerably on their walk; whether it was the fresh air that had done it, or his heavy-handed attempt at humor, Booker couldn't say. He pressed on.

"Could you tell me, anyway, a little about it all?"

"Certainly. Donald Irish provided me with a loan—or rather, his bank did. A much smaller loan than I had asked of him, which made me furious at the time, I recall. But in the course of providing the loan, or securing it, or something, he came out here and went over our books. Financial history. Assets. Operating expenses. Racing income. Stud fee income. On and on. I thought I was pretty good at that kind of thing. Hugh and I had managed well enough for twenty years."

"Not exactly, if you desperately needed a loan," Booker pointed out.

"I didn't say I was desperate. But you're right, Barnhouse needed help. We had a streak of bad luck, and there was almost nothing to cover it with. But Donald Irish was a miracle worker. Within six months he had taken our whole financial setup and kind of shaken the cobwebs out of it."

"Suddenly everything was fine?"

"No. Not fine, Captain. But at least we could go on. That meant everything in the world to me."

"I see." If Booker was surprised at this candor, he didn't let it show.

They arrived at the stable, a low, rectangular building of wood over stone, one of three such buildings grouped around a small paddock. Inside, there were six stalls. In the ordinary course of things, there were four horses regularly assigned to this building. But since the day of Willy Grimes's remarkable discovery, the stalls had been empty.

"Nobody home?" asked Booker.

"We moved them, Captain. Horses are rather sensitive, especially to a place where they have experienced terror. Hugh thought it best to put them in the foaling stable for now."

"I see. No foals?"

"Just one, and he's large enough now to run out and play."

"Uh-huh." Booker looked around for his sergeant. "Fenton?"

"Here, Chief." Mike Fenton stood up in the last stall box on the right. He had evidently been lying down, for the front of his shirt was covered with hay and dust.

"That the one?"

"Yes, sir."

Leslie Downing remained by the door as Booker advanced down the short corridor to the box where the sergeant stood. He peered in.

"Can't see much in here. Getting dark. Mrs. Downing, ma'am," called Booker, "would you have a flashlight that we might borrow?"

"How about a light, Captain?" Leslie Downing took a step sideways and reached for the wall switch. Three overhead fluorescent fixtures flickered to life.

"Much better, thank you." He raised an eyebrow at Mike Fenton.

"Will you need me any longer, Captain?" asked Leslie Downing.

Booker, who was bent over the stall railing, straightened.

"If you could just tell me one or two more things. How many horses were in here on Friday?" He walked halfway toward the door; Leslie advanced to meet him.

"Four," she said. "Including Midnight Blue."

"And what was their schedule?"

"None of that group is racing any longer. The older horses pretty much do as they please, unless they are required for stud purposes. Midnight is a stallion. The other three are geldings."

"That means they don't—"

"That's right, Captain."

"Hmm. I see. You say they do as they please. What would it have pleased them to do on Friday night?"

"They are generally fed and watered in the early evening."

"In here?"

"In here."

"Now, Midnight, he was going to race on Saturday. Wouldn't there be a special schedule for him? Plate of pasta for dinner, like the marathon runners get?"

Leslie Downing laughed gently and shook her head. "In fact, Captain, the point-to-point was going to be a piece of cake for him. It's a familiar course, and the other entrants are all, like Midnight, old hands at it. The race was not an event, Captain. Just a ritual for us all. That includes the horses."

"Yes. Yes indeed." He put up one hand and rubbed his chin, looking around. "And, speaking of that, ma'am. Of course the whole town was expecting Hugh to ride, as usual. But then we heard there was a change in plans."

She regarded the policeman steadily. "Yes."

"Care to tell me about the reason for that?"

"I don't see that it has any bearing on the matter, Captain."

"Nonetheless."

Leslie Downing sighed briefly. "Hugh is getting a little old, Captain Booker. Although he doesn't like to admit it. I was concerned. He hasn't jumped in a good long while."

"I expect that he would know if he was fit to ride, Mrs. Downing. An old hand like Hugh—kind of a devoted family retainer, in a way. He wouldn't do anything to embarrass the stables."

"Perhaps you're right. Frankly, I thought it was a bad idea to replace him. But Donald insisted."

"Mr. Irish was a riding man, then?"

"No. Scared to death of horses, would have been my guess. Although he was careful not to let on."

"I see." Booker looked at the woman carefully. "Mrs. Downing, you haven't suggested why Irish was in the stable on Friday night."

"I'm afraid I don't have a clue about that."

"But you knew he was here?"

"I didn't know he had come to the stables. I knew, of course, that he was at Barnhouse."

"For business reasons? A meeting with Hugh Shields?"

"No. No—he had dinner with me. And Peter, who was in town from Chicago for the weekend. It wasn't really dinner, just a casual supper of salad and bread. I think I gave the coroner this information on Saturday."

"Yes, well, I haven't had a chance to learn everything from him just yet. What time was your dinner over?"

"We made a very early night of it. Because of the race the next day. We finished at nine or so. Donald left about fifteen minutes later."

"Just the three of you for supper?"

"Yes. I wanted Donald and Peter to have a chance to talk."

"Any special reason for that, Mrs. Downing?"

"We were going to be married, Captain."

14

AFTER GIVING THE policemen directions to several of the other outbuildings, Leslie Downing returned to the house, leaving Booker and Sergeant Fenton to poke around as they liked. They spent an hour or so searching everywhere, opening and closing the door to Midnight's stall, sifting through scattered hay and oats and who knew what. The stable did not yield much in the way of information, however, and by seven o'clock they were through. Booker put out the light as they left.

The sun was beginning to go down in earnest now, and there were still a number of people they needed to see. Sergeant Fenton went to the car, which he had driven down to the stable, and got out a roll of yellow tape. It bore the words HAMILTON POLICE—DO NOT CROSS in heavy black lettering. They sealed off the stable and headed for a ramshackle wooden building forty yards away that served as a dormitory for several stable hands and jockeys.

This was a single-story frame structure, painted dark green, with windows running all the way around. A yellow bug light burned in a rusty fixture above a screen door. Booker knocked, and the door rattled flimsily on its hinges.

"Anybody home?"

They heard the creak of a cot. A small man with long brown hair, dressed in jeans and a Ghostbusters T-shirt, peered out through the door.

"Help you?"

"Mr. Gordon? Hamilton police." Booker flashed his badge.

"Mark's not in. I'm Jerry Ramirez. Come on in." He held the door open.

"Mr. Ramirez. I'm Captain Booker, and this is Sergeant Fenton."

"Something wrong?"

"You might say that, Mr. Ramirez. Mind if we sit down?"

He looked about the place. There were half a dozen cots, some made up, others obviously vacant. There was a sink at each end of the room, each graced with a rickety shaving mirror above; and at one side a door led off toward the back of the building—probably to a bathroom, Booker surmised. A clothesline hung limply, as if disowning its burden of mismatched socks and regrettable shirts. Ramirez had been reading; his book lay on top of his pillow. Without apology, Booker sat down and examined it.

"Like murder stories, do you, Mr. Ramirez?"

"Yeah." The jockey watched Booker carefully.

"Mickey Spillane, eh? I'd have thought you'd prefer Dick Francis."

"Not much escape in that," Ramirez said with an air of pointing out the obvious. He took a seat on a footlocker. "Besides, the hero always gets beat up bad. Something wrong?" he asked again.

"Mr. Ramirez, it has come to the attention of the police that the death of Donald Irish, here at Barnhouse, was not an accident."

"No fooling. Murder?" Ramirez looked thrilled. Fenton grinned. He loved the enthusiasm of amateurs.

"Murder, Mr. Ramirez." Booker looked sternly at him and pulled a small notebook from the inside pocket of his pinstripe jacket. "I see the idea delights you."

"What's that supposed to mean?"

"According to statements we have received, there were several people staying here at Barnhouse the evening the incident occurred. You were one of them?"

"Yes sir. I was here Friday. Came in from New York to train with Mrs. Downing on one of the two-year-olds. She was thinking about the Travers for that horse, but I told her no way."

"And why was that?"

"Slow as molasses. No—that's not fair. But not up to the Travers. More a question of nerve, a big race like that."

"Which horse is this?"

"Meretricious—the filly that won the Hunterdon Stakes last August."

"And is Meretricious one of the horses that sleeps in the barn where Mr. Irish met his death?"

"Stable," Ramirez corrected automatically. "No, sir."

"Did you have any reason to visit that stable?"

"No. Never go near it."

"How about your bunkmates?

"Probably not. At least, not on Friday. Wasn't anything to do there Friday."

"Yes, I see. Who were your bunkmates on Friday?"

"Well, Gordon—you obviously know about him. Chico Flinders, he's one of the handlers. And Scott Bauman. He's a stable hand."

"What did you do, the four of you?"

"We had some supper—there's a little kitchen next to the bathroom over there. Scotty's a whiz at spaghetti. Then we played cards."

"Poker?"

"Bridge."

"Bridge?"

"Yeah. Good game. You play?"

"Yes, I do," said Booker. He looked disconcerted, as though he might have to rethink his reasons for playing. Mike Fenton rolled his eyes. He hated bridge.

"And then?" Booker prompted.

"Well, it was the night before the Hamilton Cup, so you know, it was kind of like a holiday. We hung out. Gordon had some tapes with him, and we cranked up the music a little bit. Drank a beer."

"Until what hour?"

"Midnight, maybe."

"All of you?"

"Gordon went out."

Booker nodded and made a note. "What time?"

"Eight-thirty, nine."

"Where did he go?"

"Some chick. Said he'd be back early. I guess he went down to the Seven Locks to shoot some pool."

"But he was racing the next day."

"Yeah, but he didn't seem to be worried." Ramirez paused. "That Midnight Blue, he coulda' run the course in his sleep. We all knew that. And even Gordon had figured out that his first big race at Barnhouse was kind of a joke. Otherwise, there woulda' been a jockey. You know, a real jockey. Not a trainer."

"Have you worked with Mr. Gordon much?"

"No, sir. Seen him around, a little, like up at Saratoga last season. But we never been with the same outfit. Not till now."

"But you could sense that he thought the Hamilton Cup was a joke. You think it's a joke." Booker's tone was disapproving.

"Not a joke, really. More like fun. We all like it. But it's not serious. Mrs. Downing, she's got a real nice way of making you feel like family. She likes to get all the jockeys here for a few days each month, kinda' like under her wing, you know?"

"Isn't that rather an unusual arrangement?"

"Yeah, I suppose so." He looked at Booker for a moment without speaking. "The best jockeys, the really top best, are racing all the time. Got no time to hang out, you know? But jocks like me, maybe getting a little old or something, we don't ride all the time. It's nice, the way Mrs. Downing and Hugh work it for us. When we are between engagements, like the actresses say."

"You are paid?"

"Just a stipend, to be on call. That's what she says, 'On call.' Like doctors."

"Did Mr. Irish approve of this arrangement?"

"Got me. I doubt it. But he didn't know anything about racing, did he?"

"Did you know him well?"

"Nah. I'd seen him once or so when I was staying here. He kept a little desk in Hugh's office, used to sit in there and look over the bills sometimes. Late in the day, I guess when he got off work at his bank."

"Did you have the sense that Mr. Irish wanted to make changes around the place?"

Ramirez thought. "Hard to say. He definitely had ideas."

"But your arrangement is satisfactory?"

"For me, sure. For Mrs. Downing, too, I think. Even old jocks get around, know who's out there. And we can still ride. Kind of like having a guardian angel, or something, if Mrs. Downing believes in you. Then it's almost like old times, just maybe a pound heavier." He patted his stomach. Fenton looked involuntarily down at his own, breathing in.

"Where are your bunkmates tonight?" Booker asked.

"Scotty and Chico went down to the Seven Locks."

"And Mr. Gordon?"

"Don't know. He's supposed to be at Bowie on Saturday. We got somebody good up on Stanley Steamer. Now, that's a horse that might go to the Travers next year. Even the Triple Crown. Lotta' heart. But Gordon, I haven't seen him around since Monday. Maybe he took off already."

"Has the horse gone?"

"Tomorrow."

"I see. Well, thank you very much, Mr. Ramirez." Booker rose. "If you think of anything that may be of importance, please let us know."

Booker and Fenton stepped out into the freshening air of the evening.

"I have an idea about all of this, Mike. Right now, I'd like to know where Gordon is," said Booker.

"Do we want to see Hugh Shields first?"

Booker looked at his watch. Eight o'clock. "No, Sergeant. Let's call it a day. Your burgeoning family awaits you."

15

HAVING NO BURGEONING family of his own—nor indeed family of any kind—Fielding Booker decided to head for the Seven Locks Tavern for a chat with Flinders and Bauman. He dropped off Fenton back at the station and headed down through town to the old road that ran parallel to the disused railway, between the tracks and the river.

The road wound past many old mill buildings and loading platforms, now silent and empty, to the head of the railway canal. Here, in the old canal works building, was Nils Reichart's establishment. In spite of the dwindling economy in Hamilton, the place did a thriving business, catering chiefly to the leisure-hour requirements of those laborers who still found employment in the neighborhood.

Booker was greeted with a smoky, beery blast of air as he entered. The place seemed full for a weeknight, and the jukebox blared "Brown Sugar" as he removed his homburg and made his way through the small crowd to take a seat at the bar. Reichart nodded to him, signaling over the din; Booker pointed at the mug of draft beer on the bar next to him, then sat back and surveyed the crowd.

He soon spotted two men whom he took to be Flinders and Bauman. They had commandeered the pool table, and along with it the interest of two women in tight jeans and sweat shirts. Booker watched as one of the men took lengthy and careful aim with his cue; Booker guessed it would be a solid to the right corner pocket. The Stones' tune came to an abrupt end; and the sudden quiet in the bar must have thrown off the man's concentration. With a smooth stroke he sunk the eight ball.

"Ohh, Chico!" exclaimed one of the women. The other man laughed as the one called Chico buried his head in his arms. "Five bucks, pal," said the other man. "Next round's on me. Mags, baby." He took some crumpled money from his pocket. "I buy, you fly." He patted her bottom, and the one called Mags headed for the bar. The jukebox came on again: Van Morrison singing "Crazy Love."

"Evening, Bookie." Nils Reichart brought a big mug of beer and placed it before the policeman.

"Nils." Booker lifted the mug in greeting and took a swallow. "Busy night."

"I'll say. Usually don't get this kind of crowd on a Wednesday. Won't argue with it, though. But I wish they all had your style, Bookie." He glanced at Booker's suit. "Don't get many who dress up nice like you for a night at the Seven Locks." Booker looked at Reichart steadily. "Just finishing work?" the barman asked.

"Yes. Long day."

"Fighting crime on the streets of Hamilton."

"You might say." Booker's tone was mysterious. Reichart regarded him closely.

"Everything okay?"

Booker looked at his beer for a moment before answering. Then he gestured toward the pool table with a backward flick of his head. "Those two men. Flinders and Bauman, right?"

"Yeah. Hands out at Barnhouse."

"They come here a lot?"

"What is this?"

"Just answer the question, Nils. Please."

Reichart looked uncomfortable. "Yeah. Couple nights a week, usually. Why?"

"How about a fellow called Gordon? New assistant trainer." Reichart shook his head. "Don't think I know him."

"He was here last Friday night."

Reichart thought for a minute. "I can't say for sure. A trainer. But he rides, too, right?" He paused and looked off into the distance. "I think I might have seen him. Little guy. I remember I didn't recognize him, then I figured he was the new guy. Friday night, maybe. Or maybe it was Saturday."

"The race was scheduled for Saturday."

"Oh—yeah. Yeah! He was here. 'Cause I remember wondering why. You know, if he was gonna race. Out drinking beer the night before. Even if it was only the Hamilton Cup. It was his first time. I didn't think it was respectful."

"What time did he leave?"

"No idea. I saw him kind of early—probably about nine or so. Don't remember when he left."

"Do you think he left before closing time?"

"I think so. Fridays we close late. One o'clock. I think he was gone by then."

Booker thought for a minute. "Can you introduce me to some people here tonight?"

"Sure, Captain." Reichart looked wary. "Tracy!" he called to the barmaid. She finished pulling a mug of beer, then approached. "Tracy, would you ask Chico and his pals to join us here for a drink when their game is through?"

Through thick layers of shadow and mascara, Tracy narrowed her eyes at Booker. "Sure." She smiled at him and headed for the pool table.

"What will you have, gentlemen?" Booker asked politely when Bauman and Flinders arrived. "And ladies." The women were in tow.

"Beer," said Bauman, holding up his bottle.

"Beer all around, please, Nils." He turned to the stable hands. "My name is Fielding Booker. I am with the Hamilton Police, and I would like to ask you gentlemen one or two questions."

"Puh-leece!" whispered the one called Mags. Booker bowed.

"That's right. Miss—"

"That's Mags. Margaret Bessly." It was Bauman who spoke.

"How do you do."

"And I'm Tricia Porter."

"Miss Porter."

Patiently, Booker took the two stable hands through their

account of their activities on Friday night. It matched
Ramirez's account, but Booker noted that when the subject of
the bridge game came up, Bauman displayed very little
enthusiasm. He had been glad when Gordon left and they had
to end the game.

"Mark Gordon is due in Bowie on Saturday," said Booker.

"Yeah. For the Steamer," said Bauman, with true affection
in his voice.

"Has he left for Maryland already?"

"Don't know. I figured he was around. But I didn't see him
yesterday."

"As far as you know, did he have plans to be away from
Barnhouse this week?"

"I don't think so." It was Chico Flinders who spoke. He was
a well-built, dark-haired man in his early twenties.

Tricia Porter made a small noise.

"Yes, Miss Porter?" asked Booker cordially.

"Uh-um. Well, I—I talked to him yesterday," she said with
a defiant glance at Flinders.

"Whaddya mean, you talked to him? You don't even know
the guy." Flinders was derisive.

"Yes I do." She looked at Booker. "I met him on Friday
night. Right here." There was a momentary silence, then
Tricia Porter continued.

"I work at Steve's—the gas station with the superette. On
Long Oaks Road."

"I know the place."

"So, Mark came in and filled up yesterday. I work in the
store, not in the booth, but there's a register inside that shows
the sale. You know, for like when the booth is closed or
something."

"Yes."

"So I knew he filled up. Because I could see all the gallons,
and like how much it cost, on the register."

Gordon must have made an impression on the woman,
Booker reflected, if she had bothered to watch his tank fill up
with gas. Flinders, to judge by his expression, had reached the
same conclusion. He scowled.

"And he came into the shop?" Booker prompted.

"Yeah. Bought a lot of stuff."

"What sort of stuff, Miss Porter?"

"Oh you know, like some popcorn, orange juice. Couple of packs of gum. And a map."

"A map."

"Yeah. Illinois map. I remember, because it was the last one and later I had to send in the little order slip. You know, to get a new pack of them."

Booker was quiet. Bauman leaped at the obvious question.

"What does he want with an Illinois map—" he asked, "if he's driving to Maryland? That's the wrong way."

"Listen, mister—uh, Officer. Maybe you want to let us know why you're asking these questions?" Chico was by now in an ill humor.

"I am inquiring into the death of Donald Irish, Mr. Flinders."

"But I thought—" Flinders let his voice trail off. He got the picture. So did the others. There was a sudden, gloomy silence.

"Yes, Mr. Flinders. You thought. So did we all. It now appears we were mistaken."

He replaced his hat and headed for the door.

16

By Thursday morning, Dewey was feeling a little guilty about her treatment of Tom Campbell at yesterday's meeting. Puttering in her garden, she thrust the intrusive question of murder aside and tried to think of a solution to her professional problems. How could she make Campbell feel important without compromising the integrity of her beloved books? For she felt very firmly that encoded, magnetized, electrified strips of plastic, or whatever the things were, should never intrude themselves into Hamilton's eclectic and interesting collection of volumes.

Suddenly, however, she imagined once more Tom Campbell as a choleric infant, making speeches to his appalled mother. Dewey laughed aloud. Really! He was too Gilbertian for words. "A greenery-yallery, Grosvenor Gallery, foot-in-the-grave young man!" she sang, feeling cheered. "He will unbend himself. Or we will do it for him!"

She cut a few of the remaining bunches of lilac from a bush that grew alongside the front porch, inhaling their sweet fragrance as she headed inside. Susan Miles was coming to lunch, and Dewey was at a loss for a menu. "I am in a pickle," she remarked to Isaiah, who was lurking mournfully by an empty bowl. "A pickle." She took a vase down from a cabinet and filled it with water. Isaiah yawned and settled his huge square head back onto his front paws.

Dewey opened the icebox. "I do *have* pickles," she said. "What could I serve with them?" She hunted around in the cold nether reaches of an ancient refrigerator, rooting among lurking packages of uncertain provenance. She pulled out a foil-wrapped oblong and sniffed at it dubiously. *"Plus ca change, Isaish, plus c'est un vrai chose."* She tossed the mysterious package in the garbage and resumed her search, finally emerging triumphant with lettuce and a worn tomato. "We'll have salad!" she proclaimed. Isaish closed his eyes firmly and slept.

Susan Miles knew Dewey well and loved her quite a lot. She arrived, therefore, prepared to take her lumps in the luncheon department. She could have a sandwich later, she reasoned, surveying the rather alarmingly unorthodox salad that Dewey had fabricated. She would think of this as an appetizer.

Food, anyway, was not the centerpiece of today's program. Susan was ready to burst with curiosity about the goings-on at Barnhouse. She was dying to talk to Dewey about it all.

As the two settled themselves for lunch, Dewey tried to get her mind off murder by chattering cheerfully to Susan. "You know, Grace gave me a gift certificate for my last birthday. I found it this morning—what do you say to a little trip into town later?"

"Terrific idea," beamed Susan. "Wasn't your birthday in October, Dewey?"

"Yes, yes. It was. I'm afraid I mislaid the thing. But you know, I need your help spending it." She leaned forward and said with a conspirational air, "It's from the Negligee Nest!"

"Ooooh! Dewey! Some skimpy little silk number would be just your style." Susan laughed. The Negligee Nest was the poshest lingerie shop for many miles around. Ordinarily, Dewey never darkened its door.

"Nothing racy, Susan." Dewey looked demure. "I hear they have some nice bed jackets. That sort of thing."

"I think we'll look at the black lace, Dewey." She glanced at her friend. "But *modest* black lace," she amended.

"I'm afraid I'm not a very racy type, you know."

"Not like Mary Barstow," agreed Susan. It was well known in Hamilton that the dental hygienist was a frequent patron of the Nest. "Speaking of Mary and her would-be boyfriends,"

Susan continued, "I think there is something very strange about Donald Irish's death. I just know it."

Dewey looked at her guest uncomfortably.

"Fielding Booker was out there asking questions yesterday," said Susan, in leading tones.

"I'm sure it had to do with putting down the horse," said Dewey, her face a blank.

"Oh, come on. Since when did Leslie Downing need permission from the police to shoot a horse? Anyway. There's much more to it than that. I was at Steve's gas station this morning, and do you know what I heard?"

Now Dewey was genuinely baffled. "I can't imagine, Susan."

"You know the girl who runs the little store there? Tricia somebody. *She* saw Bookie at the Seven Locks last night. I heard her telling one of her friends on the phone. The police are trying to find that new trainer. He's disappeared."

Dewey sat back in her chair, feeling a strange sense of relief sweeping over her. Ever since she had made her dreadful calculations on the paper place mat at Josie's, she had been full of unease. She realized now that she had been terribly frightened. Frightened that the murderer was, somehow, very close to home.

"Dewey?" Susan looked carefully at her. "Are you all right?"

"Yes." Dewey smiled. "I'm feeling wonderful, Susan." She rose and cleared the dishes, coming back to the table with her gift certificate in hand. "Let's shop. And, on the way, you can tell me all about it."

When Dewey and Susan pushed open the doors of the Negligee Nest, they were greeted by a distinctly pink and pungent scent. It was as though all the bath powders and perfumed soap in the world had come to roost in Hamilton. Choking slightly, Dewey advanced with a timid air, looking about her with dismay.

"Need some help?" asked a young saleswoman.

"Oh!" said Dewey. She rummaged in her handbag and came up with a crumpled piece of paper. "Could you tell me if this is still any good?"

Smiling, the woman took the paper from Dewey and looked it over. "Sure, Mrs. James. No problem. Do you know what you want?"

"Something in black lace," said Susan.

"Susan, please." Dewey blushed. "I think I want a night-gown. But I don't want to waste that certificate on a flannel one. Something a little more exotic, I think."

"We don't carry flannel. Exotic, we've got. There's a lot on sale, you know. Have a look at this rack."

The telephone rang, and the woman stepped behind the counter to answer it. As Dewey and Susan conferred about the merits of a peach satin robe, they could hear her talking excitedly.

"Yes! Tricia says the police came to see her *again* this morning!"

Susan gave Dewey a look. "*See*. Dewey, I just know there is something really fishy about all of this."

Dewey kept her expression impassive, but listened carefully as the sales clerk talked on and on. The woman Tricia, it was clear, had been quick in getting out the word of Booker's inquiries.

"Do you think they really suspect him of something?" persisted Susan in a whisper. "Why are they looking for him if there isn't something fishy? Dewey, you must face facts."

Dewey smiled at her friend. "I *do* face facts, my dear. It's rumor that I try to avoid."

But in spite of this proclamation of intent, Dewey was burning with curiosity. Clutching the robe and a silk nightie, she approached the counter, trying to think of a way to open the subject gracefully.

"Listen, I've gotta go. Talk to you later, babes." The clerk hung up. "Sorry. Do you need me?"

"Oh, I—that is, can you show me to the dressing room, please?" Dewey asked.

"Sure." She led Dewey to a small changing room and showed her in, pulling the curtain across for her. "The satin one might be kind of nice," she called to Dewey through the curtain.

"You don't think it's too showy?" came the muffled response.

"Nah. Might be kinda' hot, though. Doesn't breathe."

"That's a point." Dewey held up the silk nightgown next to the robe. Peach and pale blue. The two might go well together.

"Hey," called the saleswoman. "Did you hear that there's a manhunt on? For some guy from out at the big racing stable, you know, Barnhouse. He split, and the police are looking for him. My friend at Steve's gas station was the last one to see him. He just took off!"

"Is that so?" replied Dewey, emerging from the dressing room and stepping up to the sales counter.

"Yeah." The sales clerk took the clothes from Dewey. "Both of these?"

Susan came over to get a good look while Dewey made her final decision.

"They're half price," prompted the woman. "You can do it with your gift certificate."

"Well, in that case, you know, I think I will," said Dewey.

"Great. So Tricia says she thinks this guy split for somewhere in Illinois," the clerk continued. While she wrote up the sale, she related Tricia Porter's tale to Dewey and Susan. "I met the guy, too," she concluded. "He was here last week. Buying some—" she looked at Dewey "—well, some pretty hot numbers."

"Your friend Tricia must have made quite an impression on him," said Susan.

"Oh, those things weren't for Tricia," said the clerk. "She'd have told me, for sure."

"No doubt," agreed Dewey. "The woman is a regular Edward R. Murrow."

"Probably out getting her license from the FCC today," said Susan.

The girl handed Dewey her package. "I think you'll like these, Mrs. James."

"Thank you very much, Miss—I'm afraid I don't know your name."

"Vikki. Vikki Rose."

"Miss Rose. I think perhaps you ought to speak to the police about your encounter with Mr. Gordon."

"You do? Me tell the police about it?"

"Yes."

"Don't you think it's kind of unimportant?"

"That's difficult to say."

"Well, maybe you're right. Okay. Good idea." She thought for a minute. "No reason why Tricia should be the only hero."

"No, indeed," agreed Dewey.

Dewey returned home greatly cheered, her arms full of beautiful lingerie and her head full of gossip. She was feeling so much better, in fact, that she was ready to concentrate on her own life again. She picked up the phone to call Tom Campbell. It was time to mend some fences.

On the drive home, she had hit on just the way to do it. A compromise that would please everyone—an amnesty program for holders of missing books. She was sure that her strategy would make Tom happy, and enable the library to recoup a part of its losses. Her light-fingered readers would gladly surrender some of their booty, Dewey reasoned, if they could do so in the dignified half-light of anonymity. And the officialese required in developing and carrying out the program was sure to appeal to Tom deeply. He could give his muse free rein, and write a stern and wordy pamphlet on the subject of what future measures might be necessary if the missing books were not returned. She telephoned him excitedly.

Tom was magisterial in his enthusiasm. "You have hit upon a marvelous initiative, Dewey," he pronounced in his round tones. "The perfect thing. When we can make the public comprehend the tremendous damage that theft does to our asset base, *then* we shall find ourselves on more solid ground. I anticipate that our plan will obviate the need for strict inter-diction, for a 'hands-on,' if you will, approach to the security issue. *If* we conceive and carry out this plan with exactly the right civic and moral tone. We must inspire both confidence and fear, I'm afraid. But I've little doubt that we shall make great strides."

As Campbell's voice droned on in her ear, Dewey opened a

can of dog food and filled Isaiah's bowl. "Yes, Tom, capital, capital," said Dewey mischievously. She rolled her eyes at the dog and tried not to laugh. "That is precisely the style of thing. You must combine a tone imperious with a demeanor nobly bland." She rang off, filled with mirth, and on an impulse phoned George Farnham, who promptly invited her to dine with him. Still feeling delighted with herself, Dewey accepted.

George Farnham was an excellent cook, even when he wasn't trying. But he had obviously made an effort for Dewey this evening, and the results were spectacular—a pasta dish with a sweet and fiery red pepper sauce, followed by an indescribably tender red snapper, and a delicate salad to close. The extravagance of the meal caused Dewey much alarm. She hoped desperately that George would not make any amorous proclamations over coffee.

As they ate their dinner she told him delightedly of her success with the Campbell initiative, as she called it.

"You'll make a politician yet, Dewey," said George.

"Never!" she responded, amused. "I'd step on far too many toes, George. And most people think I've got a screw loose. They dismiss me."

"Bookie didn't dismiss you," George pointed out.

"No, he didn't. But he's not exactly Sherlock Holmes, is he?"

"More like Kojak with hair." George chuckled.

"You should have seen him in his office yesterday, George—all official and very grand. He was very hush-hush about the whole affair. I'm not allowed to talk to anyone but you. Police orders."

"Which suits me just fine," George looked at Dewey affectionately.

"Oh, George."

"'Oh, George.'"

"Anyway, Bookie seems to have a suspect. Mark Gordon."

"The new trainer?"

"That's the one." She related to him Susan Miles's account of Bookie's visit to the Seven Locks. "It's wrong of me, I know, but I do feel better when I think it wasn't—"

"One of your neighbors."

"Yes, if you know what I mean."

"I know exactly what you mean, my dear. But the police haven't arrested him, have they?"

"No." Dewey's uneasiness began to return. "But if what Susan heard this morning is true, the man took off in a very suspicious way. *Right* at the time, too, when it began to look as though murder might be suspected."

"Could be coincidence."

"Yes it could," admitted Dewey. "But if so, it's an unlikely one. Maybe there was something in his background."

"Something illegal?"

"Yes, or immoral—that would have put him out of racing."

"And Irish found out about it."

"That's right. Perhaps he threatened to expose him."

"But it was Irish who hired him. Surely he would have found out about something like that before hiring the man."

"We only *assume* that Donald Irish hired him. Because we can't imagine that Leslie Downing would unseat Hugh on Hamilton Day."

"Good point." They were silent a moment.

"Does the library take the racing papers?"

"You mean the betting sheets? Lord, no, George."

"Hmm. Too bad. It would be interesting to do a little research."

"I'm not allowed, George. That's straight from the top. Bookie can do the research."

"Not like you can, my dear. You were born to ferret out little specks of neglected information. Nobody in the world can do it like you can." He smiled broadly.

"George." She didn't like Farnham's tone. He always flattered her when he was going to talk her into something.

"Well, say we wanted to do a little digging. Where would we start?"

"We?"

"Come on, Dewey dear. Don't pretend the situation doesn't interest you."

"It horrifies me," she said bluntly.

"Horrifies you *and* interests you, then." George removed

the salad plates from the table. "Coffee?" he called from the kitchen.

"Yes, please." Dewey's tone was abstracted. George felt pleased; she'd taken the bait.

"I'd like to know why Irish was in that stable at all," said Dewey, when George brought the coffee. "When I went out there last week—oh, it seems a year ago!—to return that currycomb, he made it quite clear that the stable was off limits."

"That's natural. Valuable racing horses."

"But listen, George—" Dewey shut her eyes momentarily, recalling the scene. "There is more than one stable building. And the good horses—I don't mean any slight to Midnight, of course—but the good horses have a stable at the other end of the paddock."

"I'm sure it's just policy, Dewey. They can't allow people in there. Strangers might bring in hoof-and-mouth or something."

"Don't be daft, George. You're missing the point, anyway. Irish isn't—wasn't—a riding man. Rob Jensen told me the other day that Irish wouldn't know a sack of oats if it fell on him."

"Maybe one did," was George's chipper reply. "The perfect weapon for a cereal murder."

"George. Stop. That's dreadful." She laughed in spite of herself. "But what was the man doing there?"

"When we know that, my dear," said George, rising, "we shall probably have our answer."

Indeed, Dewey had taken George's bait. Booker was earnest and well-intentioned, but could he handle this situation? She herself was much better suited to this kind of thing. But she would have to be circumspect. Booker had already warned her off.

As she left George's house and made her way out the long, winding course of Hillside Road, Dewey became lost in thought. She was still thinking when she went to bed, to dream uneasily of foxes and hounds.

17

WHILE EVENTS HAD thus been carrying Dewey along in their wake, the redoubtable forces of Hamiltonian justice had not been idle. Indeed, this powerful machine had begun to spread a wide and unforgiving net. In the morning, Sergeant Mike Fenton had taken down a formal statement from Tricia Porter about her encounter with the voyaging Mr. Gordon. Meantime, Fielding Booker called once more at Barnhouse. By now he was sure of his man, but he wished to make certain the trainer had not returned in the night to his rough and honest bunk.

It was most unsatisfactory to Booker that no convenient blunt instrument, covered with the victim's blood and hair and bearing the unmistakable fingerprints of a known felon, had presented itself to his investigators. The premises had been thoroughly searched, but there were hundreds of heavy things about—pitchforks and stirrups, hammers and blacksmithing tools. Everything was dismayingly neat and tidy. From this nightmarish abundance of murderous appliances, not a thing was missing. A careful forensic examination of each would take months.

Booker groaned inwardly as he considered the possibilities. There was always the chance he would strike it lucky and find the offending object before too much time had gone by. So far, however, nothing had turned up.

Nor had anyone at Barnhouse seen Gordon. Yesterday, no one had noted his absence, but recent revelations cast a suspicious light on this sudden disappearance. So on Thursday afternoon, Booker interviewed Leslie Downing once more, pressing for details of the jockey's history. She had not been able to offer much information.

"I'm sure I don't have to tell you, Captain," said Leslie Downing, pouring coffee from an ancient-looking percolator, "that your news of yesterday has caused us all great distress." She motioned him to a seat at the table in the old-fashioned kitchen and handed him a mug of coffee.

"Yes, ma'am."

"It's unnerving. Hugh is very unhappy."

"And you, Mrs. Downing?"

"I have less imagination than Hugh. I shall cope."

"Glad to hear that, ma'am." Booker sipped at his coffee. "We want to find this man Gordon."

"Yes, Captain. We all wish you would. I'm afraid nobody here has any idea where he may have gone."

"You didn't know him well."

"No. Donald—that is, we had only just hired him."

"It was Mr. Irish's idea, then, to hire Mr. Gordon?" Booker asked.

"Donald was the one who wanted to hire a new trainer, Captain," she said, "but he did not actually do the hiring. I did. Or, rather, Hugh and I. By phone."

"What kind of information did you base your choice on?"

"The usual thing. Trainers and jockeys are like horses, Captain. They have reputations in the racing world. And of course, if you're about to invest your time or money foolishly, people don't rush forward to tell you so. Until you discover your mistake."

"Then the time of the Hamilton Cup was to be a kind of probationary period for Mr. Gordon."

"Certainly."

"He had not committed himself permanently to you or to Barnhouse."

"We had engaged him for three months. Nothing beyond that."

"I see." Booker rose. "Thank you for the coffee, ma'am. I'd like to have a word with Hugh Shields, if I may."

"Certainly."

She led Booker once more through the trees and down the

small hill toward the stable area. In the late morning sunshine the horses, moving slowly about in the lovely, grassy enclosures, looked majestic and confident. Their world seemed to hold great promise.

"A remarkably beautiful spot, Mrs. Downing," Booker said conversationally.

"Yes," she answered, lightly and simply.

When they reached the paddock they found Hugh Shields mending a broken fence post. He wore a dirty baseball cap, and his ragged work shirt and jeans made a contrast to Booker's aged but still natty tweed suit.

"Morning, Hugh," called Booker as they approached.

"Hello, Bookie," said Hugh, putting down his tools and wiping his hands on his trousers.

"Like to ask you a question or two. Do you mind if we talk in your office?"

"Not at all."

"I'll leave you to it, then, Captain," Leslie Downing said briskly, striding away.

The manager led the way across the sunlit paddock into the small outbuilding that served as his office. It was dark and cool inside. Shields took a seat at his desk, indicating a small armchair for Booker. The policeman sat and looked around the little office. His gaze was transfixed by the sleek marble desk in the corner. Hugh Shields watched him.

"Belongs to Donald Irish," he said at last.

"Made himself a fixture, eh?"

"Yup." Hugh was noncommittal.

"To judge by what Mrs. Downing told me yesterday, he just about saved you all."

"He did that," Shields replied. "He was a wizard with the numbers. I don't know what he did, but it seemed like magic."

"So I've been told." Booker leaned back in his chair. "Any idea where this Gordon fellow has gone?"

"Nope."

"You saw him here last—when?"

"Monday. Sometime Monday, I think. After the funeral."

Booker sat forward. "Tell me what you know about the fellow, Hugh."

"He had a good record, not as much experience as I might have wanted. But we can't always get just what we want. Not right now. And he'd have come along."

"I see. But now?"

"I don't know. Him leaving like this; it's bad. Means he might be unreliable."

"Means more than that. He might be a murderer, Hugh."

There was silence in the little room. Booker let his gaze stray to the calendar over Shields's head; he studied with apparent interest the portrait of the lesser cloverleaf weevil.

"Did he know Irish at all, Hugh?" Booker asked finally.

"I don't know how he could. Was only here a couple of days."

"Before, I mean."

"Irish didn't know much about racing. Or riding, or horses. Not before he turned up here in Hamilton. I don't think he knew any trainers or jockeys, outside of Barnhouse."

"And there was nothing in Mr. Gordon's behavior, during the time he was here at Barnhouse, that might have made you uneasy about him?"

"No, Bookie. Not as a person. And I never really got to see him at work."

"No, I suppose not." Booker leaned forward, his arms on the desk. "Hugh, what do you think Irish was doing in the stable on Friday night?"

Hugh shook his head and looked at Booker. "That's what got me puzzled, Bookie. I can't figure it. He didn't have any reason to be in there."

"When did you last see him?"

"When he arrived on Friday. Just about suppertime. He drove down here to the paddock first, and we talked about a few things."

"About what?"

"Business. Feed orders, repairs, that kind of thing."

"Mr. Irish was beginning to take an interest in the nuts and bolts of your operation, it seems."

"In a way." Shields looked uneasy. "He wanted the billing and such to be organized differently. So he had to take a bit of an interest."

"Still, it might have felt like interference to you." Booker regarded Shields mildly. There was no reply.

"Well, I thank you for your time, Hugh. I'm sure I've kept you from your work." Booker rose, prepared to take his leave. "By the way, how's that back of yours?"

"My back? It's fine." Shields looked puzzled.

"Oh. I heard it was giving you trouble. Thought that might be why you weren't riding Midnight on Hamilton Day."

Shields shook his head. "Nope. Just thought it might be nice to let the new fellow up. Make him feel part of things. That's all."

"I see. Thank you, Hugh." Booker departed.

Booker had left his car up by the house. As he walked back up the little hill toward it now, he looked—not without envy—at the beautiful surroundings. A place like this required a huge amount of maintenance, obviously. The fences about the near enclosure were apparently in the midst of their spring repair, and they gaped forlornly in several spots. A pile of fence post timber lay at the base of the little grove of trees nearest the house. Booker strolled over and took a look.

Most of the posts were of new timber, freshly painted and placidly awaiting their installation. Booker picked through the pile. At the bottom, underneath the new posts, he found an old one. It was weatherbeaten and chipped, and bore evidence of many years of wear. It also had a small but captivating brownish stain, two-thirds of the way up, along one of the sides.

"Hot-diggedy," said Booker. "Hot-diggedy dog."

18

THUS BOOKER GOT his first piece of luck. The fence post, upon being examined, yielded human blood and skin fragments that matched the victim's in every particular. There were, of course, no fingerprints. But this didn't seem to matter. An observer might have noticed the new buoyancy in Booker's step.

He got his next break early Friday afternoon. In a small town in south-central Illinois, a plucky travel agent named Babs Palm ran across Mark Gordon's name on her computer screen. Babs Palm was married to a cop, and she liked to take an interest in her husband's work. So, happily for Booker, the name of Mark Gordon had rung a bell.

Gordon had booked two tickets from St. Louis to Baltimore. And two more: Baltimore to Jamaica, one way. After making arrangements to have Gordon flown in, Booker telephoned the woman in Illinois.

"You missed your calling, Mrs. Palm," he said warmly. "You should have joined the force."

"Glad to help, Captain. It's kind of exciting to think I ticketed a murderer!"

"You probably do it more often than you know," came the disconcerting reply. "Thank you very much." As Booker hung up, Sergeant Fenton appeared in his office door.

"Got him," said Booker cheerfully, rubbing his hands together. "Got him. My hat is off to Babs Palm, of Vandalia, Illinois."

"Yes sir. Uhh, sir—"

"Pity she's a married lady. I'd like to send her flowers."

"Yes sir. Sir—"

"Maybe I will, anyway. Well? What is it, Fenton?"

"Sir, Mrs. James is here to see you."

"Not now, Fenton."

"She says it's important."

"I said, not now, Mikey. Please." Sergeant Fenton remained in the doorway, regarding his superior stolidly. Booker gave in. "Oh, all right. All right. Send her in."

Dewey appeared moments later. "Bookie, I'm sorry to barge in on you like this."

Booker rose and gestured to the visitor's chair. "Not at all, Dewey. Not at all. But I don't have more than a minute to spare." He pulled out his pocket watch and consulted it somberly.

"I'll just take a minute." She remained standing. "I only wanted to say that I've had an idea. And there is someone you ought to speak to. About that young man."

Booker looked at her blandly. "Which young man is that?"

"Don't be cagey, Bookie. Mark Gordon, of course."

"Now, Dewey. I really can't discuss the case with you. We've been all through this. But you can relax. I have everything under control."

"But, Bookie—"

"And I have to go." He looked at his watch again. "I'm due to see Judge Pierson in fifteen minutes."

"Bookie, if you're getting a warrant—"

"Dewey." Booker's tone was firm.

"Yes, then, all right." Dewey looked at her friend. "You may want to reconsider. There are things a woman knows, that's all." Dewey gathered her purple sweater about her and took off.

Booker watched her go with relief.

"Fenton!" he shouted.

"Yes, sir!" The sergeant appeared once more at his door.

"The St. Louis police are bringing Mr. Gordon in for us by chopper this evening."

"Yes, sir."

"See that he is made to feel welcome."

"Yes, sir. And, sir, there was a call earlier from some woman who thinks she may know something."

"Don't they all. *Not now,* Mikey. We've got an investigation before us."

"Yes sir."

Mark Gordon did indeed feel welcome on his arrival in Hamilton; absurdly so. Sadly for Booker, however, the truth was not long in the uncovering.

"Well, Mr. Gordon," said Booker, when the jockey was seated in his office. "I suppose you understand why we have brought you here at such short notice."

"Nope. No idea." Gordon, a skinny, unwashed man with greasy brown curls and bad skin, slouched nonchalantly in his chair.

"Come now. Surely you remember what happened last week at Barnhouse."

"Yeah, sure. That guy got killed and all that."

"And all that. Exactly. Didn't it occur to you that the police might want to interview you?"

"Nah. What for? I didn't even know the guy."

"And didn't you know that Donald Irish's death was not accidental?"

"Yeah, there was an accident. Sure. He spooked that stallion."

"He did not spook the stallion, Mr. Gordon. Not while he was still among the living."

"Huh?"

Booker was becoming exasperated. "He was murdered, sir. Done in. Offed."

Gordon whistled. "Somebody croaked him?"

"Precisely."

Gordon was suddenly alert. "Hey, wait a minute. You think *I* did it? No way, Jose! You gotta be kidding."

"Mr. Gordon, let's start with the obvious here, if that will please you. Would you care to tell us—me and my sergeant here—exactly why you left Hamilton in such a hurry for Vandalia, Illinois?"

"Sure. To get married."

Booker groaned. "Dewey James!" he muttered. Fenton closed his notebook with a sigh.

For form's sake, they questioned Gordon closely about his movements on Friday evening. He had remained at the Seven Locks until slightly after midnight, talking and drinking beer with the increasingly cheerful Tricia Porter. Then he had driven back to the Barnhouse. He had noticed Donald Irish's car, parked down by the paddock, but had thought nothing of it. And he had noticed no disturbance in the stable block, nor lights of any kind.

The two police officers took Gordon carefully through the events of his journey and his nuptials. He had not mentioned his marriage to the people at Barnhouse because he didn't know them well enough. And, Booker reasoned, Gordon probably didn't wish to put off the comely Miss Porter. A little mystery with regard to his conjugal status might prove pleasurable to him in the coming months in Hamilton. In the event that his happy bride did not make an immediate appearance on the scene.

A dejected Booker sent Gordon on his way.

"We're back at ground zero, Mike," remarked Booker.

"Not quite, Captain. We've got the fence post."

"We do. You, me, and the fence post. Run along home, Mikey."

As he locked the door of the police station behind him, Booker heard a cheerful greeting.

"Hello, Bookie," said George Farnham.

"Hello, George."

"You're looking a bit green about the gills."

"I'm not surprised that it shows, George."

"Well, come and have a drink, then, and tell Uncle George all about it."

"Thank you. I'd like that," replied the policeman. They strolled peacefully along Howard Street toward the river, in silent enjoyment of the warm evening air. Summer wasn't far off, and the quickening insect life had begun to hum and chirp.

They arrived at Farnham's house. Within, there was a cool,

clear, spare feeling. Booker left his hat on the rack in the hall and followed George into the living room.

"Now, let's have it," said George, when he had poured out their drinks.

"I'm afraid that Gordon fellow didn't do it, George."

"Oh, no. You've found him then."

"We interviewed him this evening. He hasn't got an airtight alibi, but I'm fairly convinced he had nothing to do with it."

"Why did he run, then?"

Booker laughed. "He was running to the arms of his loved one. He ran to join his intended in holy wedlock. Or not-so-holy." He related the interview to Farnham. "Poor Babs Palm will be disappointed."

"That his girl?"

"No, that's the clever travel agent who found him for us. Thinks she issued tickets to a murderer." He laughed again.

"Don't spoil it for her, Bookie."

"No, I won't." They chuckled. Booker was suddenly serious. "You know what this means, don't you?"

"I think I do."

"Yes. I'm afraid all of this is a bit closer to home than we'd have liked to think."

"No possibility of an intruder?"

"It's unlikely. For a variety of reasons. The place isn't exactly a fortress, but there are a few dogs around. According to the staff, the dogs do a good job of keeping strangers away. Besides—" he paused to take a long pull at his scotch, "the whole thing feels like an inside job."

"Because of the location of the body?"

"Let's just say that I have a feeling. When you've been in this business long enough, George my boy, you get a sense of these things." George ignored this last remark. Booker continued.

"Plus the clumsy attempt to pass it off as an accident. Almost anyone could have spotted that setup." Booker had the grace to avoid meeting George's eye. "I will tell you, in confidence, George, that there were very few signs of a struggle at the scene. Someone knew the lay of the land pretty well." Booker looked hard at George. "There is one person we haven't talked to yet." He nodded with an air of mystery.

"Peter Downing," said George.

"The son and heir. That's right. It's time Mr. Downing paid another visit to his mother." He rose. "Thanks for the drink, George." Booker took his leave.

19

YOUNG WILLY GRIMES was a remarkably good worker. He had visited Midnight Blue at Dewey's place for a week now, and each morning had done a little in the way of making small repairs and organizing Starbuck's stable. Early on Saturday morning he showed Dewey the most recent transformation he had wrought in the tiny outbuilding.

"If you keep things like I fixed 'em up for you, Mrs. James, it'll be a lot easier." He indicated a small shelf, newly erected, which now bore all of Starbuck's liniments and other equipment. These Dewey privately thought of as horse cosmetics.

Dewey was overcome. "Thank you so much, Willy. I hardly think I deserve this state. But Starbuck does. Both the horses do, and for them, this is paradise enow. On their behalf, I thank you." She bowed gravely.

"It's okay." Willy grinned and stroked Starbuck's nose and opened her stall door. The mare sauntered out into the warming late spring sunshine. Willy cast a regretful look toward Midnight. Under the terms of his reprieve, the stallion was confined to quarters.

"I'm sure they miss your influence at Barnhouse." Dewey regarded with admiration the new shelf Willy had built. Ranged on its surface was quite an assortment of currycombs— the new one that Dewey had bought alongside several others that the boy had unearthed in his excavation of Starbuck's lodgings. "You must be quite an asset to Hugh," she went on. "Nothing out of place there, I'll bet."

"Not a thing," answered Willy proudly. Their morning

106

routine of feeding the horses, followed by breakfast in Dewey's kitchen, had created a strong bond of companionship between them. "Mrs. James," he continued in a more serious tone, "is it okay to ask you about something?"

"What's that, Willy?"

"Is it true that Mr. Irish was murdered?"

Dewey took a deep breath. "Yes, Willy, I'm afraid it's true."

"That's what I figured. Wow." Willy hoisted himself up to sit on the stall railing. Midnight nudged him with his long, sleek nose. "I knew you didn't do it, Midnight." He stroked the horse's silken cheek. "I figured it was murder, Mrs. James, when the police came to see me. The captain came," he added importantly. "But he said he was only like investigating." Willy looked at Dewey. "Do the cops know who did it?"

"I don't know, Willy. I think they have some idea."

"Captain Booker asked a lot of questions. All about Friday night, when Mr. Irish died."

"I imagine he would need to take a statement from everyone who was there."

"Yeah." He thought for a moment. "Hey, Mrs. James. I need to ask you something else." Willy hopped down from the railing and stood facing Dewey, his hands in his pockets.

"Yes, Willy." Dewey plumped herself down on a bale of hay and rested her chin in her hands.

"Let's say you had to tell about something that might get somebody in a whole lot of trouble. Would you do it?"

"Had to tell? You mean there was something about Barn-house that you had to tell Captain Booker?"

"Yeah." Willy dug a toe into the dirt.

"I think it's always best to tell people the truth. And if it's a question of murder, you know, then it's really your obligation to make as full a statement as you can." She looked up at Willy. "Want to tell me about it? Sit down." She patted the bale of hay next to hers. Willy sat.

"You know, Mr. Irish always thought I was making trouble."

"He did?" Dewey's mind flashed back to her encounter with the man, ten days ago. She recalled the scene between Willy and Irish that had been taking place when she'd arrived at Barnhouse.

"Willy," she said, "do you remember when I came to return that currycomb?"

Willy laughed. "Sure, Mrs. James." His eyes flickered toward the new shelf he had built.

"You were upset about something," said Dewey.

"Yeah. Well, see, that's it." Willy's face flushed angrily. "That guy," he said enigmatically.

"Mr. Irish?"

"Yeah. He was always saying when anything went wrong that it was my fault."

"It's just your age. That point of view is an unfortunately common one, Willy. One day you will learn to keep your head when all about you are losing theirs." Willy looked mystified, but Dewey was unfazed. She had grown accustomed to blank stares from her interlocutors. "What I mean is, don't take it personally. What was the problem that day?"

"Something about the feed." Willy looked uneasy. "There was something in it."

"Something in it? What do you mean, Willy?"

"I didn't want to tell the captain, 'cause I don't want to get anyone in trouble, Mrs. James."

"I doubt if you've made trouble for anyone. You have my word, Willy."

"Somebody had put buttercups in it."

"Buttercups!"

"Yeah. Just a little. Just enough to make the horses not want to eat. They don't like buttercups."

"Indeed they don't. But they might have become ill." She mused. "Was there somebody at Barnhouse who liked to play practical jokes, Willy?"

"Nah. But Mr. Irish always thought it was me."

" 'Always.' You mean it happened more than once?"

"Yeah. Well, not the buttercups." He looked carefully at Dewey. "There were a couple of weird things. When Mrs. Downing would be away or something. Like when the girth on one of the saddles got shredded."

"Oh, dear me. Did anyone get hurt?"

"No. But they might have. And Mr. Irish thought I did it."

"When did this happen, Willy?"

"The week before."

"Do you know who was responsible?"

"No. Honest."

"What other things like this happened, Willy?"

Willy scratched his cheek thoughtfully. "There was a problem one day with Meretricious. She got lost. But we found her all right, somebody had just let her out when she should have been being groomed." He looked glum. "I had to tell the captain all about it." They sat in silence for a moment. "We went out there, and I showed him around the tack house and everything, showed him how I left stuff."

"Was it all the way you had left it?"

Willy laughed. "No. I'm the only one who puts things away right. But it was weird about the blanket."

"What blanket?"

"Midnight's. It wasn't there anymore. And I know that nobody would want it, because it was supposed to be mine. Like a souvenir thing, you know, after the race." Willy looked annoyed.

"I'm sure it will turn up, Willy."

"Yeah."

"Willy. You left Barnhouse after dark that night, is that right?"

"Yeah."

"Did you see anything unusual?"

"No. Well, it was pretty dark. I took the shortcut across the south pasture, down to the front road, you know?" Dewey nodded. "And I stopped to lift my bike over the fence and I saw somebody walking across the paddock."

"What time was it?"

"About nine-thirty or so. I had to be home by ten."

"I see." Dewey stared blankly in front of her. "Who was it, Willy?" she asked finally, in a soft voice.

"He was too far away."

"But?"

"He was too far away," said Willy firmly. He stood.

Dewey roused herself. " 'The one of them said to his make,

Where shall we our breakfast take?' Come and have something to eat, Willy," she said, with a cheerfulness she did not feel.

Dewey was lost in thought as she did the breakfast dishes. Willy had departed, full of indifferent pancakes and delicious speculation about murder. But the boy's revelations had left Dewey nervous and disquieted. She was not so concerned with ferreting out who it was Willy had seen that night; the police would find out, through one means or another.

She was worried, however, that Willy might be in some kind of danger. Had he been seen by the murderer?

And Dewey had been right: there *had* been something wrong at Barnhouse. If it turned out that Booker was right about Mark Gordon, then the pranks weren't connected to the murder. But Dewey felt that there had to be a link.

George had pooh-poohed her intuition, but Willy's story bore it out. A prankster—whose goal was what? To make Hugh Shields look like a bad manager? Who would want to do that?

It could have been Irish. And yet, Dewey recalled, Irish had appeared quite upset about the adulterated feed the day she had seen him at Jensen's Feed & Grain—for this was clearly the issue that had prompted the acerbic exchange she had witnessed. It was unlikely that Irish had altered the feed himself; unless he hoped to cover his tracks by making a complaint to the merchant. That seemed awfully byzantine, even by Dewey's rather roundabout standards.

She wondered briefly if she should talk to Fielding Booker about the episodes. There was no indication that the practical jokes, if you could call them that, had anything to do with the murder. Besides, the police thought the murderer was the Gordon man. Dewey had intruded far enough òn police territory, she told herself. Booker would not be happy to see her again at headquarters.

Just as Dewey reached this point in her considerations, the telephone rang.

"Dewey, it's George."

"Yes, George. Hello."

"I thought you might be interested in a little piece of news I heard last night."

"Well, George?"

"The police found Mark Gordon."

"Oh. Oh, I see. But he—do the police have a case?"

"Afraid not, my dear," replied George. He told her about Booker's visit last night.

"So he eloped. I thought as much," said Dewey.

"You did? Dewey, be serious."

"Yes I did, George."

"Booker told you."

"No, I—er, I had a feeling, that's all."

"Been talking to that horse again, Dewey?"

"Don't be ridiculous, George. I just found a clue when I went shopping yesterday."

"Shopping?"

"Yes." Dewey felt her cheeks grow pink. "At—at the Negligee Nest, George, if you must know."

George gave a wolf whistle.

"Stop that this instant, or I won't tell you."

He stifled a chuckle. "All right, my dear. Sorry. Fill me in."

So Dewey filled George in on her conversation with Vikki Rose.

"Why didn't you tell Bookie?" asked George when Dewey was through.

"He didn't want to hear about it."

"Inspector Clouseau strikes again."

"Yes. I'm afraid so. But George, why didn't everyone at Barnhouse know, too?"

"Seems our Romeo didn't want to share the news of his bright hour in the arms of Venus."

"Don't muddle your allusions like that," said Dewey automatically. But her mind was only half on George's solecisms. She was in truth disturbed by his news. "Thank you for letting me know, George."

"Can I persuade you to come out in my car for a spin this afternoon, Dewey?"

"What's that? Oh, no, George. Thank you. I have a million

things to do. And so do you. Are you ready for the rezoning meeting on Monday night?"

"Mmm. Thanks for the bleak reminder."

"I'll see you then, George. It will be quite an interesting time." She rang off.

News of Gordon's release started the wheels churning again for Dewey. It would be best to talk it over with Booker some more. But she knew that she was making a nuisance of herself. She would have to think it through on her own.

She could not shake the notion that there was a connection between the strange goings-on at Barnhouse and Irish's death. Had anyone talked to the people at the bank where Irish worked? Surely the police had done so, she reflected. Or what about people from Irish's past life, including his ex-wife? Dewey shook her head. This was a local business, Dewey felt. It had Hamilton at its heart. It had Hamilton by the throat.

Dewey made up her mind to take action. She climbed into her weather-beaten station wagon and headed to Barnhouse, determined somehow to put her mind at ease.

Hugh Shields was busy giving instructions to one of the grooms when Dewey drove up. She climbed out of the car and headed across the paddock to where the two men were examining the near hind hoof of a beautiful bay gelding.

"Okay, Scott, that'll do," Shields was saying. "Let me know when Tack Marvin gets here. If that hoof doesn't have time to heal, Our Man Fritz won't race this year at all." He sent groom and horse on their way. "Morning, Dewey."

"Hello, Hugh," said Dewey warmly, shaking his hand. "Are things settling down here a bit?"

"Look to be," said Shields, shaking his head. "This has been quite a week for us. Terrible business. But I'm trying not to let it interfere."

"Well, everything certainly looks shipshape to me." Dewey looked around appreciatively.

"We'll be back to normal soon," said Shields. "What brings you out?"

"I've come about the horse, Hugh. I thought we ought to

talk. He's awfully valuable, you know, and I just thought we should discuss the situation."

"Sure thing, sure thing. Come on in." He led the way across the paddock to the business office.

Irish's marble-topped desk and halogen lamp were gone, and along with them any hint that there had been an offering made, on these premises, to propitiate the demigods of contemporary design. In place of the banished furniture stood stacks of old magazines and breeding records. These had been relegated to a hayloft when the fastidious banker had appropriated a section of the office. The place looked more like itself, now that he was gone.

"You have quite a resource in that young Willy Grimes," Dewey began.

"That we do," agreed Shields, scratching his head. "Sit down, Dewey, sit down. Yes indeed, he's a terror for neatness, that boy."

"He has positively transformed Starbuck's stable this week," she said with a smile. Shields chuckled, and little wrinkles appeared at the corners of his eyes.

"Better watch yourself, Dewey, or he'll be down at the library next. Give that pie-faced Tom whatsit a run for his money."

Dewey beamed. "You know, Hugh, you're a genius!" She cackled with delight and her eyes danced. "We happen to need a volunteer for our Juvenile Readers Committee."

"Hoo, boy!" said Hugh, deeply amused. They giggled.

"Now, Hugh, about Midnight Blue," said Dewey, recovering herself. "What am I to do?"

Shields shook his head. "That's up to the boss. But I'm afraid the picture looks black." He regarded Dewey carefully, his eyes sad. "It was awful nice of you to step in the way you did, Dewey."

"To make intercession for the transgressor? I know I'm a busybody, Hugh, but I'm glad I did."

"He's a good old horse, is Midnight. The whole thing is really a shame."

"Tack Marvin will have to change his opinion, Hugh."

"I dunno. I sure hope so, Dewey. I haven't been able to get

Mrs. Downing to talk about it yet. I expect we'll be making arrangements to bring him back here, no matter what. But you understand that she was kind of laid low by this whole business. She loves that horse, Dewey. It will be damned tough on her, if he has to be put down. I'd rather put it off."

"Certainly, Hugh. I will be happy to let things ride for another week or so, until Leslie can focus on it all."

"I can let you have a bag of feed, Dewey, if you'd like. I'll get Jensen to bring one by."

Dewey arched a brow. "That would be nice, Hugh. Ask him please to hold the buttercups."

Shields looked at her gravely a moment, then leaned back in his chair. "Willy tell you about that?"

"Yes."

"Irish thought Willy had done it. Wanted to fire him. I had a time talking him out of it."

"Who do you think the culprit was, Hugh?" Dewey asked in a soft voice.

"Some kid from around. You know how they can be, sneaking in at all hours to play a trick."

"I suppose you're right. Somebody was meddling with Starbuck's stall door, and I had the same thought exactly." Dewey rose to take her leave. "By the way, shall I send Willy here tomorrow after he stops by my place?"

"That would be nice, Dewey, thank you. I miss the little tyrant. This place is a wreck without him."

He rose and showed Dewey to her car.

20

FIELDING BOOKER WAS discouraged. This morning, as he donned his best-loved weekend togs—corduroys, a pale blue cashmere sweater, and an old tweed jacket with elbow patches—he thought about the Irish murder. It was a great pity for all concerned that Mark Gordon had turned up innocent. For if you must have a murderer in your midst, it's far nicer if he is not counted among your friends.

Booker's blue mood, however, had a certain grim substance to it. It was of a sustaining nature, generating enough will to carry him through a joyless task. This morning he would see one or two people who worked at the bank with Irish. The bank employees had all given preliminary statements, shortly after the murder was discovered, but Booker hoped to uncover some sort of intricate, out-of-town business affair that might have caused the man's undoing. Because the alternative was decidedly upsetting.

Like most of those in Hamilton who watched the unfolding drama, Booker felt in his heart that the murder was a Barnhouse affair. Unlike his neighbors, he would not be able to turn aside, merely appalled by events. He was compelled to apprehend the murderer, destined by his place in society to see justice done.

He opened an old pine chest and rummaged around in the bottom, emerging at last with a misshapen lump of tweed. It was an old deerstalker, which his sister had sent to him when he earned his detective's shield. Twenty years ago, now, at least. The hat smelled like mothballs. He smoothed it and

115

clapped it on his head, then went to take a good look at himself in the mirror.

"Elementary," he muttered to himself.

Feeling idiotic, he tossed the deerstalker aside and set off to see Marjorie Mole, now acting manager of the Warren State Savings and Loan.

Marjorie Mole was a tall, rather fleshy, nervous woman who lived in downtown Hamilton, not far from her office at the bank. Her apartment was dark and depressing, overrun with small pink items and bad reproductions of indifferent artwork; the whole was overlain with the cloying scent of a fetid potpourri. When Booker arrived, she had insisted on making tea. This turned out to be a vile, flowery-scented brew, which she served up from an ornate and hideous pot into matching cups and saucers.

Booker had been warned about Marjorie Mole's habit of laughing at the wrong moment. Sergeant Fenton had described how she'd giggled upon hearing that Irish had been murdered. This morning she sat facing Booker, pinkly prim in a huge, chintz-covered wing chair.

From its depths she had listened wide-eyed to Booker's patient questions. Her responses, for ten minutes, had been unhelpful, almost obstructionist. Most were punctuated with a chuckle. Booker, perched uncomfortably on a wobbly ladder-backed chair, wondered idly if Marjorie Mole was mad.

"No, Captain, nothing irregular that I know of." Laughter. "But you see, I was not on the loan side. I'm operations."

"The only loan officer, then, was Mr. Irish."

"That's correct." She stifled a giggle and refilled her cup with more of the odious tea. Booker looked with detached revulsion at her fleshy pink hands as she lifted the teapot.

"You knew very little of the business between your bank and Barnhouse," he said.

"Between Mr. Irish and Barnhouse." She looked at her feet.

"Are you making a distinction, Miss Mole?"

"Well, certainly, Captain." She raised her beady eyes to meet his. "There was more to managing the Barnhouse money than that loan Donald Irish made." Booker waited for her to go on, but she evidently expected to be spoon-fed.

"What other kinds of things, Miss Mole?"

"Payroll accounts, for the trainers and stable hands. We took care of that."

"I see. Did Mr. Irish manage those accounts?"

"No."

"Who does manage them?"

"I do."

Booker sighed. This woman was beyond dreadful. He could not believe she was as stupid as she seemed. "Miss Mole, have there been any transactions on those accounts that seemed irregular to you?"

"Our account information is confidential, Captain." She smirked demurely and permitted herself a small giggle.

"Miss Mole!" Booker stood, towering over her. "If you please, I am investigating a murder. The murder, in fact, of your supervisor. I am surprised to find you so reluctant to cooperate. But I assure you," he thundered, leaning close to her, "that I will persuade you. I suggest, madam, that you cooperate. For your own good," he added darkly.

He turned and walked to the window, looking out between the leaves of a stringy spider plant to the quiet street below.

From within the embrace of her wing chair, Marjorie Mole began to sniffle. Poor Captain Booker! He waited for the sniffles to subside, fighting off an impulse to flee.

Finally the wing chair was quiet. He turned to her.

"I'm sorry, Captain," said Marjorie Mole. "I'll tell you anything you need to know." She smiled thinly, like one in great pain from an unfair and debilitating illness. The woman was almost certainly out of her tree.

"Thank you, Miss Mole." Booker took his seat again. "Now, is there anything that took place at the bank recently, anything remotely related to Mr. Irish, the Barnhouse stables, or the payroll accounts, that raised the red flag for you?"

Marjorie Mole thought. She sipped her tea. She thought some more, and then finally shook her head.

"Nothing at all, Captain. Except, of course, for Friday."

"Do you mean yesterday?"

"No, last Friday."

"The day of the murder?" Booker's voice rose an octave. Lord, what a woman!

"Yes. When Peter Downing was in town."

Booker held his breath.

"He closed his account with us, you see, and withdrew everything."

"A lot of money?" Marjorie Mole hesitated. "Miss Mole!" Booker roared.

She quivered. "Yes, a lot. I think it's safe to say that it was more than ten thousand dollars."

"How did he take the money?"

"In a certified check, made payable to him at a bank in Chicago."

"Was this sudden?"

"Yes."

"How long had he held the account?"

"It was in trust for him for many years. And we held it just the same, after he moved to Chicago."

"Now, Miss Mole, I want you to think very carefully about what happened that day. Was there any sign, any little clue, why Peter Downing might have wanted to do this? Think carefully, now. Any little thing you may have overheard could make a difference here."

She stared back at Booker with yellowish eyes.

"Who gave him the check?" Booker shouted.

"I certified it."

"Did he speak to you or explain the withdrawal?"

"Not exactly. No. And, well, I can't say for sure, but I think it had something to do with the argument."

"Peter Downing had an argument, Miss Mole? With whom?"

"Why, with Mr. Irish, of course." She looked at Booker, blinked, and giggled into her handkerchief.

"Fenton!" Booker roared as he strode hurriedly into the police station. "Fenton!"

"Here, sir." Fenton appeared in the doorway to his office.

"Fenton, get Peter Downing on the phone." Booker headed for the coffee pot in the corner, whose thick and murky brew he hoped might prove an antidote to the perfumed tea of Marjorie Mole.

"Just spoke to him, sir. I told him we could go there to see him, but he said it would be easier the other way. He'll be down this afternoon."

"Good work. Ugh. I feel like I need a bath." He shuddered and took an enormous swallow of coffee. "Whew!"

"Something wrong, sir?"

"That Mole woman." Booker shot his cuffs. "At least she gave me something."

"Cooties, sir?" asked Fenton with a grin.

Booker shuddered again. "Do I smell like violets to you, Fenton?" He extended a lapel for his subordinate to sniff.

"More like lavender, Captain. It'll fade. What did she have?"

Booker grew suddenly serious. "Peter Downing had an argument with Donald Irish on the day of the murder. Right at the bank."

Fenton whistled. "About what?"

"His mother, would be my guess. The Mole isn't sure. Or if she is sure, she isn't sure she should say. What a morning." He sat down heavily in the chair behind his desk. "But apparently Peter Downing spent about fifteen minutes with Irish in his office, and there was a heated exchange. Raised voices behind the closed door, the whole thing. When he left Irish's office he closed a large account that he'd had with the bank for years. Money his father had given him in trust, when he was still a kid."

"Why didn't she tell us this before?"

Booker looked at his sergeant closely. "It seems there are hidden springs in our Miss Mole. I finally pressed the right button."

"I don't want to hear about it," said Fenton with a laugh.

21

IT WAS NEARLY eight on Saturday evening by the time Peter Downing's plane from Chicago touched down at the little Hamilton airport. Booker awaited him in the office, having sent a grateful Sergeant Fenton home an hour before. "Go and see if your wife still loves you, Mikey," Booker told him. "Lord knows I don't."

Downing climbed out of a taxi at the station and presented himself to Booker. He looked cool and unruffled, and decidedly amused. Booker did not like his attitude.

"Thank you for coming, Mr. Downing." Booker indicated a chair for him.

"Glad to oblige, Captain. I felt I owed my mother a visit, anyhow. She is tough, but not accustomed to murder on the back forty." He sat with a graceful motion and crossed his legs. "I was surprised to learn that Irish had been murdered."

"Yes. Hmm." Booker consulted a file briefly, then looked up. "You were present at Barnhouse the night the incident took place."

"Yes."

"It was your first visit in a long while, was it not?"

"That's right. Never did like horses, really. Not a country boy at heart, I guess you'd say."

"Do you mind telling me what brought you home that weekend?"

Downing uncrossed his legs and straightened them before him, plucking a tiny piece of lint from his knee. "It's a good question, really, Captain. I'm not sure I have an answer for you. Let's just say that I felt it was time to visit the homestead." He allowed himself a lopsided grin.

"Were you checking up on things, Mr. Downing?"

Downing frowned politely. "I suppose you might say that."

"And one of the things you were looking into was your mother's relationship with Donald Irish."

"Hasn't a man the right to be curious, Captain? Without straying into Oedipal deeps?"

"Certainly he has a right, Mr. Downing. I would be curious if I were in your place. Here's a stranger with a toehold in your inheritance, so to speak. Or more than a toehold. Got a foot in the door." Booker leaned forward across his desk. He made a gesture, pushing at the air. "Door about to swing wide open, let the stranger in."

"I'm not so sure I'd agree with that analysis, Captain. My mother is remarkably self-possessed." Downing slouched in his chair, relaxed.

"Is that so?" Booker leaned back, crossing his arms over his chest. "Well. We shouldn't speculate." He paused briefly. "Your mother has told me, Mr. Downing, that you and she had dinner with the victim on the night he died."

"That's right. He came to supper at Barnhouse."

"And what did you make of him?"

"Sir?"

"What was he like, what did you think of him?"

"I thought he was a rather pathetic man. Sycophantic. Charming, of course, and intelligent enough. But rather a puppy dog around my mother."

"And how did you read that?"

"Trying to ingratiate himself." Downing laughed harshly. "How he tried!" He looked suddenly grave. "But he didn't know my mother, Captain Booker. She can't be talked into liking anyone, not even for her own good." He smiled. "Not even, necessarily, her own flesh and blood."

Booker brooded, looking carefully at Downing. "What time did the dinner party break up?"

"I can't be sure. That is, I went out for a walk after dinner."

"Leaving Irish and your mother alone?"

"Yes. I thought she'd be safe enough. She never misbehaves on the eve of a big race, Captain."

"What time did you go out?"

"About nine o'clock. I'd had enough."

"And where did you go?"

"I climbed up Smallpoint Hill, the hill behind the house, to the top."

"And did what?"

"Lay on my back and counted the stars."

"How long did you stay there?"

"Don't know. A while, maybe forty-five minutes."

"Wasn't it cold out?"

"No. I do know enough to put on a jacket on a spring evening, Captain."

"So you returned to the house about ten o'clock."

"Not directly. I stopped by Hugh Shields's place. You're right, Captain, it did get chilly. Thought I'd ask him for a spot of his good whiskey."

"Kind of late to go calling."

"In the country. I'm a city boy, though. I don't get up with the horses in the morning. Perhaps I forgot my country manners."

"How long did you stay there?"

"I didn't stay."

"Why not?"

"As you have pointed out, Captain, it was late. Hugh was asleep."

"You woke him?"

"There is a shred of civility clinging to my person, Captain. No. I did not rouse him from his peaceful slumber. I merely saw that there was no welcome lamp burning in his window."

"So you don't know if he was home."

"Hugh doesn't cavort on the eve of a race, either, Captain. He was asleep. Take it from me."

Booker made a note. "How far is it from Hugh Shields's house to yours?"

"Half a mile, maybe. A ten-minute walk."

"Did you encounter anyone?"

"No."

"And when you returned home, Irish had left."

"That's right. Or rather, I assumed he had. The lights were out, except for the front hall. His jacket was gone from the little bench by the front door. My mother's bedroom door was closed, and I expect she was asleep."

"And what did you do?"

"I went to my blameless sheets, Captain."

Booker sat up and consulted his file once more. Then he made several more notes. Time passed conspicuously in the little office, as vague sounds of passing cars drifted in from the streets.

"There was more to your visit than familial pleasure, I understand," Booker said finally.

Downing stretched in his chair. "The race, of course. Old friends. Hail fellow well met, and so forth."

"Business as well, I understand."

Downing looked at Booker coolly, but did not respond.

"Oh, come now, Mr. Downing. Hamilton is a very small town. I know you had business to do."

"I did pay a call at the bank, that's true."

"On Friday afternoon."

"Yes."

"Where you had, by all accounts, a heated exchange with a man you had never met."

"I don't know how it has been reported to you, Captain. I'm sure your witnesses are credible."

"I spoke with the assistant manager. A Miss Marjorie Mole."

Peter Downing let out a hoot of laughter. Booker ignored this response and continued.

"She reports that there was an acrimonious exchange between you and the dead man."

"She should have stayed in her little Mole-hole."

"And that you subsequently closed an account at the bank, withdrawing a sum that has been described to me as 'well over ten thousand dollars'."

"That's correct."

"For what purpose?"

"Oh, really, Captain. That's my business."

"Very well." Booker leafed through a small notebook. "Would you mind describing for me the content of your conversation with Mr. Irish?" he asked, keeping his eyes on the pages of the notebook.

"It was private, Captain."

Booker lifted his gaze to meet Downing's. Then he put the notebook down gently. "Nothing is private in a murder investigation, Mr. Downing."

There was a long silence.

"Mr. Downing, what was the subject of your dispute with Irish?"

Downing crossed his ankles and gazed at his feet. "I wanted to discuss some matters having to do with the management of Barnhouse."

"Oh, really?" Booker leaned back in his chair, crossing his arms behind his head. "I thought you had given up the sporting life, Mr. Downing." There was a pause. "Why did you think the running of Barnhouse was any of your business?"

"Because the 'business', Captain, does not belong solely to my mother. I have a small share."

"I see. Go on, Mr. Downing. Tell me what aspects of the business you were concerned about."

"The man was a fool!" Peter Downing said hotly. "He knew nothing about racehorses, nothing about operating a stud farm. He was a sordid little idiot bean-counter."

"Very galling, I'm sure, to those who worked for your mother." Booker stroked his cheek placidly. "And to you, too. Not surprising. I'd like to know, if you don't mind, exactly what it was—what the management difficulty was. It is critical to give the police all the information we require. Even if it doesn't seem important to you."

Downing leaned forward in his chair, arms on his knees, and rubbed his forehead. Then he looked up. "I didn't like the way the man was behaving. The lord of the manor business. And, frankly, I had the impression that something was up."

"What?"

"I don't know, exactly. Just a feeling, as I say. I concluded that Mr. Irish had outgrown his breeches, and I decided to let him know, firsthand, as a member of the family and a partner in the business, that he was to keep his plump and dreadful paws off the horses."

"What exactly didn't you like, Mr. Downing?"

"The feel of the place."

Booker sat back with an easy manner in his chair. "You are a sensitive young man, Mr. Downing. You can pick up on these feelings, even when you have been away from a place for half a dozen years."

"Perhaps I have a sixth sense," Downing replied blandly.

"You heard something."

"Nothing concrete."

"What about the new man, Gordon? Was he part of what bothered you?"

Downing looked warily at Booker. "I suppose so. He was green, but I resented his attitude. And he and Irish seemed to be hand in glove. I thought he was probably crooked."

"Did you speak to your mother about your concerns, before starting an argument with Irish?"

"I asked my mother about her plans for Gordon."

"And?"

"She refused to give me a straight answer."

"What exactly did you ask her?"

"I think I said, 'Mother, who's the nitwit that keeps pestering the grooms?' Or words to that effect."

"I see. And, perhaps not surprisingly, your mother brushed you off."

"That's right."

"So the next day you went to the bank and picked a fight."

"I didn't pick a fight."

"Very well. You had words."

"We had words."

"Perhaps you told Irish to go to hell," suggested Booker.

"Of course I did," said Downing. "That was the very first suggestion I made, Captain. There were others, I promise, that were far more colorful."

"Picture this," said Booker, leaning back in his chair, making a little frame with his hands. "Angry young man arrives home to find a stranger in charge of his family fortune. The stranger is, according to the young man's lights, a nitwit.

'A sordid little idiot bean-counter.' Tut, tut. Angry young man storms in to confront the stranger, who winds up dead. Who was, by the way, about to marry the young man's mother."

"Marry her?" Downing laughed hard. "Come on, Captain, you've been listening to Doris Bock and the Tidal Wave gals again."

Booker's surprise showed on his handsome face. "You didn't know, Mr. Downing?"

Downing laughed again. "Captain, I promise you my mother would never have married that worm."

"She told me so herself, Mr. Downing," said Booker very quietly.

Peter Downing was suddenly still. "You're joking."

"I'm not joking."

"Well, well." He looked thoughtful. "I had no idea she would go to such lengths." He shook his head. "That puts a different face on things, doesn't it, Captain?" Peter Downing nodded to himself. "I guess that makes me the surprise favorite in the Homicide Stakes."

22

By Monday morning, the word had spread like a contagion that Peter Downing was suspected in the murder of his mother's suitor. The actual facts of the case had not been discovered by the citizens of Hamilton, but the eager watchers brushed aside this trifling consideration. Doctors and lawyers, beauticians and morticians, performing artists and members of the press, as well as clergy and teachers, poets and athletes— all had heard about the strange turn of events. Some of them, practitioners perhaps of some ancient cabalistic rite, merely responded with a deep nod when they were given the news. They seemed to have known it all along.

No arrest had been made, but this was small potatoes. Hadn't Captain Booker requested that the young lawyer not leave town? Downing had obligingly secured himself a room at the Hamilton Inn, where he bore surprisingly well the careful surveillance of the town's citizenry. Under the circumstances, of course, you could understand his not wanting to go home to his mother.

In the excitement, the burning issues of daily lives faded to unimportance. At the library, where the prison literacy-for-work exchange was about to go into effect, Tom Campbell almost forgot to be sententious in his morning speech to his staff. At the Tidal Wave, Doris Bock put blue henna on a young girl who was about to be married, and had to devote two hours to administering an emergency rinse. Rob Jensen spent the afternoon at the Seven Locks with Nils Reichart, completely forgetting his appointment with the dentist, Dr. Langford. This omission, surprisingly, did not upset little Mary Barstow, Dr. Langford's hygienist. She would simply have to call Jensen later and remind him. This evening, maybe. She rather liked Rob Jensen. In the meantime, she wondered deeply about the murder.

Where others were content merely to gossip and nod, Dewey James leaped in to talk and to question. She had always been this way; it was constitutional. She did not think of her activities as bearding lions in their dens; she perhaps did not think much, one way or another, before plunging ahead. She liked to take her opportunities where she found them.

Thus it arose that, encountering Peter Downing over the shampoos at the drugstore late on Monday morning, Dewey was prompted to speak to the celebrity pariah of Hamilton.

"Hello, Peter," she said bravely.

Peter Downing turned to her. "Mrs. James." He looked at her gravely. "You'd better be careful talking to me. I may be dangerous."

"Peter, I'm so sorry about all of this."

"Are you? I'm not."

Dewey was flustered. "Well, yes. Of course I am."

"Can't say that it makes much difference to me."

"Peter, don't talk like that."

"No. It isn't the done thing, I'm sure. How is Grace?"

"She's well, thank you. Please don't change the subject—that's not what I mean, anyway. I'm not talking about appearances." Dewey looked around her. "Peter, I'd like to talk to you." The woman behind the lipstick counter was watching them. "Not here." She glanced at her watch. "And I have to be at the library in ten minutes. Could we meet in an hour or so, somewhere private?"

"Private?" Downing was puzzled but amused. He asked in a loud whisper, "How about my hotel room?"

"That will be perfect." Dewey shot a look at the woman behind the cosmetics counter. "The Hamilton Inn?" she asked in a loud voice. "I'll meet you in your room at twelve-thirty."

Dewey left Peter Downing at the drugstore and headed for the library. She was to meet with the first prisoner from Calvert, reporting to go over the details of the exchange program. Her mind was on Peter's strange attitude as she mounted the stone steps to the little turn-of-the-century library building and pushed open the familiar wood and glass front door. She breathed in deeply, welcoming the satisfying and much beloved scent of the books.

"Ah, Mrs. James," said Tom Campbell from behind the counter. "Here she is now, Mr.—ah—"

"Keith. Alastair Keith." The man Campbell had addressed turned to look at Dewey as she made her way to the counter.

"Good afternoon, Tom." She turned to Keith. "Good afternoon."

"Mr. Keith, may I present our Librarian Emeritus, Dewey James. Mrs. James, this is Mr. Keith. He is one of the con—ah—recruits, the new recruits, for our literacy program."

"How do you do, Mr. Keith." Dewey shook his hand. If she were surprised by his appearance, she did not show it. He was a tall and rather good-looking man of fifty-five or so, with impressive gray hair and bright blue eyes. He wore no prison stripes, but mufti that consisted of a tweed sport coat, necktie, and khakis. The only indication of his status was a huge ankle bracelet, with a small radio transmitter attached to it. "So glad to meet you."

"Glad to be here, Mrs. James." He spoke with a faint trace of a British accent. "We have a small library at—at Calvert, but it can't hold a candle to yours. Mr. Campbell's program is inspired, don't you think?"

Dewey suppressed a smile. "Indeed. Mr. Campbell's tenure has been a breath of fresh air."

Campbell cleared his throat nervously. "I had just embarked on an explanation of the various resources of the library. Perhaps you would finish showing Mr. ah—Keith around, while I attend to some of the back orders, Mrs. James?"

"Certainly, Mr. Campbell," said Dewey mischievously. She turned to Alastair Keith. "I'll be glad to. Mr. Keith—perhaps you would tell me a little bit about yourself first? And what you are looking for in our program?" Dewey led the way to a small table in the reference section, and they sat down.

"Well. Perhaps I should tell you, right from the start, Mrs. James, that I do know how to read. That is, when I heard about the program, I decided to see if I could be part of it, in an administrative fashion, don't you know. I have a good deal of experience in that way."

"Oh yes?"

"Yes. That is to say—look, Mrs. James, I'd like to be frank with you. If I may."

"By all means." Dewey leaned forward eagerly.

"The ah—reason, the reason for which I am currently resident at Calvert is that, for quite a long time in fact, I was engaged in a rather deplorable career."

"The law?" asked Dewey brightly, with an impish smile.

Keith laughed. "No, not as bad as all that." He took a deep breath. "I perpetrated a series of frauds on unsuspecting investors. Made quite a lot of money, as you may imagine."

"A confidence man?" Dewey was all enthusiasm.

"Yes, more or less, but cut from the corporate cloth." He began to relax somewhat. "Didn't think I was really hurting anyone, you know. Well, you know how that is."

"Yes," agreed Dewey. "If you're only taking a little here, a little there, and you don't see them cry . . ."

"Exactly."

"And—if I may ask, Mr. Keith—how long will you be staying at Calvert?"

"Oh, yes. If I behave myself, I should be at liberty to resume some sort of normal life in another three and one-half years."

"Oh, my," said Dewey. She thought of Midnight Blue, imprisoned in a stall for a crime he had not committed. Three and a half years of incarceration would probably leave him lame. If he survived it. "I suppose that seems an awfully long time," she remarked sympathetically.

"Yes, it does rather. That is why, when I learned of your project, I was eager to take part. Provides me with a welcome change of scene, and a chance to be of service to someone other than myself."

"I see. Well, Mr. Keith, perhaps you can tell me just what sort of contribution you would like to make to our program."

"I thought that, as I am qualified to be a reading instructor, I might offer to teach some of the ah—free citizens of Hamilton who may lack those skills. In exchange, I will organize the project from the Calvert side, and provide some of the necessary security support that you require."

"That would be most generous of you."

"Believe me, madam, when I say that I would welcome the opportunity to be of service. And, as a trusty of Calvert, you see, I have a certain amount of stature with the authorities, and am closer to my fellow inmates. Which will help in getting the program off the ground."

"That would be helpful," Dewey agreed.

"Yes. My idea was to organize a buddy system. In this way, one of my—er, fellows from Calvert would come with me once a week to the library. He then could receive instruction from your committee and work as a guard, as well. The Calvert officials like us to do things in pairs, anyway. It's easier to count by twos." He smiled, and Dewey laughed.

"I am flattered that you have given this so much thought, Mr. Keith. We will all benefit. Now. When will we be able to begin?"

"I believe that Mr. Reichart has arranged for the exchange to be fully underway next week. He will let you know the details."

"Marvelous, Mr. Keith." Dewey rose. "I thank you. Your enthusiasm will certainly be an asset to Mr. Campbell's program."

Feeling pleased all around, Dewey left the library and headed for her rendezvous with Peter Downing. Alastair Keith certainly promised to be an asset to the program; and his orotund manner, not to mention his British accent, would assure him a place of honor in the small constellation of people who earned Tom Campbell's approval. As she made her way to the Hamilton Inn, she cackled gleefully, imagining the two men discussing "litch-ra-chure" over tea in the small staff room. "And make each prisoner pent," she sang, "unwillingly represent, a source of innocent merriment, of innocent merriment!"

Dewey was still humming to herself as she entered the faded elegance of the Hamilton Inn. The hotel lobby was like a stage set for an Edwardian drawing room; in its ancient armchairs, such travelers who still made their way to Hamilton were wont to sit and read, or drink a cup of surprisingly good tea. Peter Downing was waiting for Dewey in a large rose damask wing chair. He collected his room key and they ascended the grand old staircase, covered in a worn but still lovely carpet patterned with huge chrysanthemums.

"We climb the rounds of life's long ladder, one by slippery one," said Dewey inconsequently as they mounted.

"Robert Browning," said Peter.

"Yes," said Dewey. Peter, she remembered, had always been a great reader.

They reached the door to Downing's room. "Here we are, Mrs. James. It's humble, but I like to call it home." Peter tossed his jacket on the bed. Dewey looked around. Downing was obviously dedicated to his work; on the desk were several files, and next to them a portable fax machine. He followed her glance. "Yes, I came prepared for a visit of several days. All my toys about me. Have a chair." He pulled up a little chintz-covered chair for Dewey and elongated himself gracefully on the bed. "I await your pleasure."

"Oh, Peter, do stop. Please. I am not here to be impressed by your cool savoir-faire, nor by your wit under pressure." She looked at him somberly. "This is a very grave situation, Peter."

"And your response is to make a secret rendezvous with a murderer?" Peter laughed and kicked off his shoes.

"Don't be silly. I don't believe for a minute that you're a murderer. I should think any fool could see that."

"Then old Bookie must be nobody's fool, Mrs. James." Downing sat up and looked at Dewey intently. "Here's what he has on me. One: I turned up at home to find that a persistent oaf had had his way with my mother. Two: Said oaf had been given free rein with the family fortune. Meaning *my* fortune, Mrs. James; or at least, my putative inheritance. Three: I had a bitter quarrel with the deceased. Four: I have no alibi for the time of the murder; instead, I took an unsubstantiated nature walk on a cold, windy night with a storm threatening. Five: I am the person with the most to gain by his removal." Downing smiled. "Quite a tidy little case."

"Peter, I do believe you're being self-important."

Whatever rebuke Downing had expected from Dewey, this clearly was not it. He looked at her with genuine amazement.

"Stop thinking of yourself, for a change," Dewey went on severely. "You always were caught up in yourself." She shook her head. "Peter, you know your mother far better than I. Yet even I have a sense that she'd not be likely to make over her fortune—her life's work—to someone who strayed across her path."

"You call marrying her 'straying across her path'?"

"Call it anything you like. Your mother is a steely woman. Not the sort to give away the shop. And I doubt she mixes affection with business."

"I wonder if she mixes affection with anything, if it comes to that," said Peter, half-smiling.

"In the course of a remarkable day, I have heard many things. I happened to have business at the bank this morning, and you can imagine the great discussion that took place. The assistant manager, that Badger woman—"

"Mole. Marjorie Mole. Yes, I heard she had uttered a squeak from the dank depths of her darkened burrow."

"There's no call to be unkind, Peter. Miss Mole naturally took center stage this morning at the bank. So by now, everyone knows about Friday afternoon."

"Oh, you mean Doris Bock was at the bank today, too?"

Dewey ignored this remark. "The entire population of this town has heard that you 'quarrelled with the deceased,' as you so engagingly phrase it." Dewey leaned forward and gave Downing a penetrating look. *"And what of it?"*

"I don't get you, Mrs. James."

"My point is this. What is Irish to you, or you to Irish, that you *shouldn't* quarrel? You see, it strikes me as rather normal, given the circumstances. Whereas murder is not normal." She sat back and folded her hands primly in her lap. Downing laughed aloud.

"I do declare, Mrs. James. I always thought you were the bright light in Hamilton." He laughed again.

Dewey went on. "Another point that strikes me in your favor—or against it, it all depends on how you keep score—is that this quarrel took place at the bank. In broad daylight, in the presence of witnesses. The only mystery is that Miss Mole should have been so long in mentioning it."

"Took her a few days to dig out."

"Peter." She looked at him reprovingly but had to stifle a laugh. "Seriously, now, I wonder. If I were in your shoes and wanted to challenge my mother's suitor, I would choose a more private venue."

"Like the stables."

"Yes, since you mention it." Dewey's eyes sparkled. "But if I were a young man with a business matter to discuss, I should do it in business hours, at a place of business."

"The bank."

"Yes, the bank, since that was Mr. Irish's principal place of business."

"Presumably, however, Mrs. James, the business I may have wished to cover was related to my own interests in this town—i.e. Barnhouse. Why shouldn't I wait to see him there?"

"Because there is someone at Barnhouse you didn't wish to offend."

"Aha! So we're back to my mother again."

"No, indeed." Dewey shook her head vigorously. "No, we are not. I have never known you, Peter, to shy away from giving offense to your mother. If you'll forgive my pointing it out."

Downing sat forward with his arms upon his knees and looked carefully at Dewey. "You interest me strangely. Go on."

"That leads me to conclude that there is someone else at Barnhouse whose feelings you wanted to protect. You were thoughtful. You wished to spare him the embarrassment of being the center of a bitter argument. Your business with Irish concerned Hugh Shields, naturally."

Downing stood up suddenly and walked over to the small washstand in the corner. "Like a drink, Mrs. James?"

"No, thank you, Peter."

"Don't mind me." He took a bottle of bourbon from a suitcase and poured himself a large shot.

"I'll continue, then, if I may," said Dewey firmly. "I imagine, Peter, that it didn't take you very long to get the measure of things. I don't mean about your mother and Donald Irish. I mean the threat to your friend, Hugh."

"How's that, Mrs. James?" Peter idled back over to the bed. He had recovered himself, and now lounged gracefully once more.

"Had we but world enough, and time, your coyness, Peter, were no crime." She looked at him sternly.

"Andrew Marvell."

"Yes." Dewey leaned forward again, regarding Downing intently. "Don't bother trying to keep it up, Peter," she said urgently. "I'm afraid it's far too late to do him any good. You must come clean."

Peter took a sip of bourbon and looked at Dewey thoughtfully. "All right, Mrs. James. You win." He sat up straight. "Here is what happened.

"I overheard Irish and Gordon in conversation on Thursday. But even before that, I knew something was wrong. I went to see Hugh on Wednesday night, when I got to Barnhouse, and he wasn't himself."

"How do you mean?"

"Distracted. Unhappy."

"Did he talk to you about it?"

"No. But I could see he had something on his mind."

Dewey nodded.

"Well," Peter went on, "I was curious. Not that I've been much of a help around Barnhouse in the last few years. I don't think Hugh ever got over my leaving. I let him down terribly." He gazed straight ahead into the empty air before him. "Still, it should have been fine. Everything should have been all right. My mother is extremely capable. And Hugh was the best thing that ever happened to her." His face was a blank.

"What did you find out, Peter?" Dewey prodded gently.

He roused himself. "On Thursday, I was in Stable Three; the one we call Victory House."

"Is that the stable where Irish was killed?"

"No. That's Horseflesh House." He laughed. "Hugh's name for it." He chuckled.

"And what happened in Victory House?"

"That's where Meretricious is stabled. You know, the remarkable filly." Dewey nodded. Downing went on. "Irish was in there with Gordon. And I heard him say something about not worrying, he'd sort Shields out, make sure he understood how things would be."

"Who said this? Mark Gordon?"

"Yes."

"What did you think he meant, Peter?"

"I assumed he was talking about racing. About racing and money."

"Fixing a race, in other words."

"That's it." Peter looked up at Dewey. "That would have been too much for Hugh, Mrs. James. He couldn't take that, being forced into that." He laughed. "Hugh's rather old-fashioned in some ways. It would have killed him."

"Well, you know, Peter, there was a victim."

Peter Downing nodded. "The grave's a fine and private place, Mrs. James," he said, unsmiling.

23

WHILE THE SYMPATHIES of the town were thus caught up with the fate of handsome young Peter Downing, Fielding Booker betook himself once more to Barnhouse, with Sergeant Mike Fenton in attendance.

It was true that Booker had asked Downing to stay on a few days in Hamilton; but the policeman was very far from having any proof whatsoever in the matter of the murder. All he had was a fence post; and this interesting artifact, while it bore bloody proof of the commission of the crime, had not yielded further information upon the minute examination by the forensic science lab.

Booker was fairly sure he had his man. But he needed more facts. And in his discussions with Sergeant Fenton one might have detected a hint of preoccupation, as though he had a disturbing notion at the back of his mind that he felt bound to explore.

Fenton was at the wheel of the police car as he and his superior made their way up the long reach of the lower drive that led to the paddock area.

"I wonder, Mike," said Booker, "whether there isn't something we've been overlooking."

"I don't think so, sir. The problem is there's nothing there to overlook. What have we got? A few statements from people. Leslie Downing went to bed at nine-thirty. The grooms were in their bunkhouse, all but Gordon, who was busy making an impression at the Seven Locks. Peter Downing says he counted the stars."

"Not that the stars will confirm it for him," said Booker firmly, "but we can't prove otherwise." He looked out the window as the car moved up the road between two vast enclosures. In the fields, the beautiful chattel of Leslie Downing grazed peacefully in the afternoon sunlight. "Lot of money out there, eating grass," Booker pointed out.

"Yes, sir." Fenton thought for a moment. "And if we believe Leslie Downing, it would have belonged to Irish."

"Not necessarily."

"But if—"

"Lord, Mikey, I declare you're old-fashioned! This is the twentieth century. Wife doesn't have to give the joker two cents if she doesn't want."

"How about alimony?"

"That's just speculation. It's not relevant." The car slowed and they pulled up at the stable block in front of the paddock. "Mike," Booker said, "I wonder about that blanket." He climbed out of the car and leaned on the open door, looking out at the green fields of Barnhouse.

"The boy's souvenir thing?" asked Fenton, getting out of the car. He closed his door.

"That's the one. Any luck tracing it?"

"No, sir. Last time anybody saw it, it was in that little house." He nodded toward Willy Grimes's proud bastion.

"The tack shed. Did you ask the staff about it?"

"Yes sir. Matter of fact, Hugh had been looking for it himself, he says. To give to the boy."

"And nobody could find it."

"No. It's disappeared. Why do we want it, sir?"

"I was thinking. It would be a pretty handy way to transport a body, in the absence of a gurney. We'd better go over every inch of this place."

"Where do we start, sir?"

"Why don't you take the little house?" Booker replied with a chuckle, slamming his car door shut.

In the business office, Hugh Shields was straightening out some accounts. An observer might have sensed an air of finality in his actions. With a pencil between his lips, he reached out for his sturdy old adding machine. Chink-a-chink. Chink-a-chink. Chink-a-chink-ching! He made a note of the sum in a ledger book and turned his gaze to the photographs on the wall.

There they were: the great and the nonstarters, side by side, the glorious beloved of Barnhouse: Our Man Fritz, Laura Baby, and Suzy Egg Business; Octavian, Uncle David, Most Likely, and Wilson's Variety; Midnight Blue, Stanley Steamer, and Meretricious. This spectacular filly was perhaps the most beautiful of them all, but not necessarily the best loved. She had been photographed in the winner's circle at Hunterdon; next to her was a proud Leslie Downing, accepting the silver cup from the steward.

Hugh Shields looked down at his hands.

"Afternoon, Hugh." Fielding Booker appeared in the doorway.

Slowly, Hugh Shields raised his eyes. "Bookie."

"Mind if I come in?"

"Nope. You're very welcome. Sit down, sit down." Shields seemed to recover himself. "What brings you here this afternoon?"

Booker sat and leveled his gaze at Shields.

"Or shouldn't I ask?"

"Hugh." The two men regarded each other. "Busy?"

Shields looked at the desk before him. It was full of ancient notebooks, wherein were recorded the fleeting and well-compensated passions of the Barnhouse stallions.

"Just looking through some old records."

"I see you've done some rearranging." Booker let his glance wander to the far corner, where Irish's desk had stood.

"Wasn't any need for that anymore."

"Back to the old order of things?"

"Not quite."

"Everything all right, though?"

"It all looks in order to me." Shields leaned his elbows on his cluttered desktop, pushing aside a sheaf of papers with one arm. "I don't know how he did it, but that man saved our necks."

"Abracadabra."

"Something like that." Shields scratched his head.

Booker leaned forward and rested his elbows on Shields's desk. "If I were in your place, Hugh, I might have thought it was all a bit much."

"It was all right with me," said Hugh unconvincingly.

"At the business end."

"That was his end. He was good at it."

Booker straightened. "Peter Downing is in town."

"Yes, I heard."

"He says he came to see you on Friday night."

Shields looked puzzled. "No, Peter came by on Wednesday night. Came to my house, had a drink. I'm sure that was Wednesday."

"Yes. Well, he came again on Friday. The night of the murder."

Shields was silent.

"At least, that's what he says." Booker stirred restlessly. "I thought maybe you could confirm it for me. He says your lights were out. He thought you were asleep."

Hugh looked Booker straight in the eye. "If that's what Peter says, Bookie, I'm sure he's right. As a matter of fact I think I did hear someone outside, just as I was heading to bed. What time did he stop by?"

"About nine-thirty or ten, he thinks. Couldn't be sure. Were you at home all night, Hugh?"

"I may have stepped out for a minute. Probably did. I usually go out for a breath of air."

"To check on the horses, perhaps?"

"No. Just for air."

"Did you encounter anyone?"

"No."

"See any lights on, in the stables, anything out of place?"

Shields sighed. "No, Bookie. No." He rubbed his chin. "It's all in the statement I gave your sergeant."

"And you didn't see Peter Downing at your place between nine-thirty and ten?"

"Like I said, Bookie. I think maybe I heard him come by."

"I know he's an old friend, Hugh." Booker rose and moved closer to the wall, looking at the photographs of the Barnhouse horses. "Quite an establishment, Barnhouse." He turned and looked at Shields. "Quite a business you've built up over the years. A great deal of know-how, determination, and guts."

"What's the point, Bookie?" Shields sounded weary.

"Tell me about your staff." Booker sat down again as Shields threw him a look of impatience. "Honest? Capable?"

"Come off it, Bookie. Of course."

"Good at their jobs. And well supervised." Booker leaned in. "Tell me, then, about the possibility that someone at Barnhouse was fixing races."

"You're dead wrong about that, Bookie." Shields looked angry. "Barnhouse is clean. We may not be the best racing stable in the world, but we're clean." He looked at the policeman. "If Leslie Downing were interested in the easy money, *Captain*, I don't think she'd have found herself in financial trouble."

Booker nodded. "The same thought had occurred to me. But I wondered about this miracle fix of Irish's. I wondered how come it was so easy, all of a sudden, for a gringo like that to make this place run smoothly. Struck me as odd."

Shields nodded, but did not reply.

"Well, then," Booker went on. "Another thing that seemed strange was the way he hired that new trainer, Gordon."

"Leslie Downing hired Gordon, Bookie."

"So I've been told. And you didn't know anything about him, did you, Hugh?"

"I didn't know him personally. But I checked up on him, all right. Talked to his references. Talked to people around."

"And there was no indication, from any of them, that Gordon wasn't clean?"

"No."

"Then why would Peter Downing, who was only here for two days, think he was crooked?"

Shields stared blankly before him for a long moment. Then he rose, shaking his head. "Bookie, I don't know. I can't help you. I've told you everything I can about the man." He moved toward the door. "Besides, said Shields, as he headed out into the sunshine, "I thought you had cleared Gordon."

Booker stood up and followed. "Of the murder, yes. There's

no reason to think he had any motive. But we're checking into that young man's background." He fell into step with Shields and they headed across a small meadow toward the paddock. "He may have been deeply in debt. Might have owed big money, Hugh, to the kind of people you should never borrow money from."

"I had no idea," said Shields. They had arrived at the paddock. "No idea."

"Why should you? I just wonder how young Peter figured it out so fast. Well, Hugh, thank you for your time." Booker's tone was discouraged. "I'm afraid we're going to have to disrupt your routine a little further in the coming days. Sergeant Fenton and one of the officers will be back again to go over the place thoroughly once more."

"Help yourself, Bookie," said Shields.

"We'll try to be discreet about it. Looks like you've got a lot to do. You probably won't even notice we're here."

"If you need me, I'll be out there." Shields pointed to the direction of the huge northern enclosure. "Mending the fences."

Booker looked at Shields oddly, and took his leave.

24

HIGH UP IN his office on the fourth floor of the Grain
Merchants' Exchange, George Farnham was buried in work.
He had not heard the scuttlebut on Peter Downing; and even
had he been apprised of the latest development in the case, he
would scarcely have had time to speculate about the young
man's guilt or innocence. Farnham was busy preparing for
tonight's town meeting—which would start in half an hour—
and the great rezoning debate.

The two hundred and fifty acres of farmland that were the
subject of the proposal lay just north of the town center, but
still within the town's incorporated district. A developer
proposed to turn the lush acreage into a residential hot spot,
with accommodations ranging from small condominiums to
full-blown houses. The battle promised to be fiery, and the
mighty forces of historic preservation had been gearing for
war. George Farnham, however, knew that people tended, in
the end, to vote their pocketbooks. He had little hope that the
land would be preserved in its pastoral purity when the
powerful persuasions of the purse came into play. In other
words, there was a lot of money at stake.

He was deep in thought over a deskful of documents when
the door to his office burst open.

"George!" Dewey was nearly out of breath. "Hello, I do
apologize for busting in on you. but have you *heard*?"

"Hello, Dewey dear," said George, rising. "I declare you're
winded! Goodness me." He bowed elaborately and escorted
her to a chair. "If *madame* would care to catch her breath?"

George chuckled as Dewey plumped down in a guest chair. "Now, what's all the excitement?"

"George, Peter Downing is back in town. At Bookie's request, it seems."

"I think I did hear the young fellow had turned up. Lending a hand to his bereaved mama, no doubt." George's tone was ironic. He sat back down at his desk.

"No. Not at all, I suspect. He has taken a room at the Hamilton Inn." Dewey was pensive. "I don't think he loves his mother much, George, but I would be surprised at his going so far to interfere."

"Why is that?"

"I think it would require too much of his precious time."

"Ooh. I see. He may be lazy, but he's not a murderer. That it?"

"More or less. I don't know." She thought for a moment. "Why do you think the police let Mark Gordon go, George?"

"Eh?" Farnham was flipping through a large file folder, his mind half absorbed by its contents. "Oh, Gordon. But I told you, Dewey, when I called you on Saturday. He went off to get married. Nothing sinister in that. Not as a rule." He chuckled.

"I am not convinced." Dewey rested her chin in her hands. "George, this is terrible. I don't say I ever liked Peter Downing, but I can't believe he's a killer."

"Why not? Because he was at school with Grace? All the best murderers were schoolmates of somebody, Dewey." But Farnham looked at his friend tenderly. "Mustn't let sentiment cloud your reason, my dear."

Dewey looked up at George, a strong light in her eyes. "It's not sentiment, George." She shook her head. "I keep thinking that there is some quite logical and orderly answer to this whole question."

"I'd say that a young man's resentment of his mother's grasping beau has a great deal to recommend it, logically."

"Oh, George, stop." Dewey stood up and began to pace the small office. "There's no earthly reason for that boy to do such a thing. It's not as though he'd have to see much of Donald Irish. Peter is almost never here."

"Doesn't he have a share in the business still?"

"Yes. But that's irrelevant and immaterial."

"Dewey, you sound like Perry Mason." George rose and began to gather up papers into a large accordion file. He glanced at his watch. "Come along, my dear. I'll take you to a show and will make you forget all this murder." He stood by her chair, watching her.

Dewey took a minute to respond; she was lost in thought. "A show? George, there isn't time before the meeting. Besides, there isn't a show in town." Her brow furrowed.

"The meeting, Dewey dear, the meeting. Plenty of entertainment in store, sure to brighten this dull evening. Shall we?" He gave Dewey his arm, and they advanced in a stately manner down the old marble staircase.

The main hall of the Exchange building was enormous, with a vaulted ceiling supported on four sides by grand arches of red granite. It was here, in days gone by, that farmers had brought large carts laden with the bounty nurtured in a generous land, to be inspected and haggled over by merchants from ten different states of the Union. The shouted testimony of these men to the excellence of their crops had echoed from the great stone walls, and the vast space had rung with the satisfying clink of money as it changed hands.

Tonight's throng was less cheerful. They seemed to have divided into two distinct camps. The preservation crowd, with a vanguard of several stout women, stood in sorry ranks about a folding card table near the front of the room. Men in wrinkled tweeds and young women in comfortable-looking clothes handed out sheets of paper to all who approached. These pamphlets were of the decidedly homemade sort, carefully photocopied onto two sides to save money and paper.

In folding chairs on the other side of the hall, also near the front, sat two smooth men and a woman of thirty or so, who managed to look both stylish and serious. They were in perfect control, lean and suntanned and healthy, gleaming with power. They were dressed as though for an important business meeting, which meant that they were certainly overdressed for tonight's affair in Hamilton; but the fine tailoring and neat accents of their clothes, the overall composure of their appearance, gave them the aspect of people whose victory was a foregone conclusion. They had attracted a small crowd of landowners, who hoped to get rich at their hands.

"There they are, Dewey. The sharks." Susan Miles nudged her friend. Susan had arrived at the same time as Dewey and George, and the two women sat in folding chairs close to the front of the hall. George took a seat temporarily in the row in front of them.

"The minions of Mammon," agreed Dewey. "They certainly look successful, Susan." There was a note of doubt in Dewey's voice. "Maybe you're right, George. Sentimental attachments won't stand a chance in the face of all that temptation."

"I'm a cynic, Dewey dear. I think that any John Doe who is offered a fortune for his fallow fields would be impractical to refuse." Farnham sounded resigned.

"Oh, George, you don't really believe that?" asked Susan.

Farnham nodded. "Not to say I think it's right. The tide will turn again, you know, and people will wish for it back."

"What's done cannot be undone," said Dewey.

"No," agreed George. "And I hear there is presently a lot of interest in selling out. Money in the bank, you know." They looked across the aisle at the well-groomed trio.

"They certainly make the preservation group look like hayseeds," admitted Susan.

The advantage held by the executives was soon undermined, however, by a serious tactical error. Dewey watched with interest as the good-looking blond man on the end of the row reached down beneath his folding chair and came up with a shiny black box in his hand. He opened it. He punched at it. Then he put it to his ear, and began to speak into it.

"Oh, really!" said Susan Miles. "Who is he trying to impress?" She giggled. The man's actions had attracted the attention of many people in the room, and some began to snicker. The hopeful landowners looked disconcerted; some gazed at their shoes in embarrassment.

"I'd like to know who he's talking to," said Farnham. "Whole damn town is here. Nobody left to call."

"His imaginary friend," suggested Susan.

"Perhaps he's soliloquizing," said Dewey. "To buy or not to buy." Susan Miles laughed again.

The man seemed to sense that he had become an object of derision. He looked around at the crowd behind him and spoke hurriedly into the phone. Then he put the thing away and leaned across to make a comment to one of his colleagues.

George Farnham glanced at his watch. "Time, ladies." He walked over to the podium and twisted the microphone, prompting the loudspeakers to a harsh screech of protest.

"Good evening, everyone." There was a stir of voices and the scrape of metal against stone as people claimed seats in the folding chairs. "Thank you all for coming." He looked out into the crowd. "I can see this is an important event for all of us. Lot of us here tonight; that's good." The clamor in the room began to die down.

"Now, before we begin, I'd like to introduce the representatives of the Aviance Realty Investment Trust, whose proposal we are here to consider." He indicated the smooth rank in the front row. "Mr. Robert Browning; Mr. George Eliot; and Ms. Elizabeth Bennet." They stood in turn and nodded.

"Those names must be made up!" giggled Susan to Dewey.

"Using undetectable aliases," responded Dewey with a laugh, "to conceal their true identities."

"As you know," Farnham went on, "they have expressed a desire to purchase property, contingent on the rezoning of that property for development purposes." He outlined briefly the proposal that the developers had made, producing a large map of the area. The property under discussion was marked in pink.

"The town zoning board members are here tonight to answer your questions and hear your points of view, of which I am sure there are a good many." Polite laughter. "I will act as moderator for the discussion, and I would like to ask you all please to show a little restraint in the expression of your opinions. This is Hamilton, after all, and not the O.K. Corral." More polite laughter.

George opened the floor for discussion. Dewey listened with half her mind. Robert Browning? George Eliot? Elizabeth Bennet? She stifled a giggle and tried to pay sober attention to the meeting. She wasn't much good at this sort of thing, she knew. There were too many distractions, and it was difficult to take people seriously in such a setting. Everyone had an axe to grind; almost everyone wanted to talk just to hear the sound of their own voices. She thought of Tom Campbell and laughed aloud.

"Dewey!" Susan whispered, reproving her friend with a nudge. One of the preservation ladies had taken the floor, and was demanding to know how the developers planned to atone for the loss of two hundred years of Hamilton history. Someone countered with a shouted accusation that the only people who cared about preserving the past were the idle rich.

The discussion went on, and on, and on. Dewey yawned. George Farnham shot her a look from the podium, where he was desperately trying to ease the contentiousness on both sides. "I think it's time we moved on to the next question. Yes, Mrs. Downing?"

There was a sudden stillness in the huge hall.

Leslie Downing was standing at the back of the rank of chairs. "Can everyone hear me?" she asked, in a calm, deep voice.

There were murmurs of assent as the crowd turned to gape. Really, thought Dewey, we are too ghoulish. But she could not help herself. She stared along with the rest of them.

"I think it's time we put aside the ideological debate and raised a few practical issues. There is one that I particularly wish to bring to your attention." She looked at the crowd. "I think most people here tonight are aware that my property lies in the middle of the proposed development area. And I am very well acquainted with the water tables, the sewage outlets, and other hydromechanical amenities and difficulties of that small area. Mr. Browning, whichever one you are—" she glanced without interest toward the Aviance group—"I think you should explain how you propose to provide adequate water for residential properties there." There was a stir of interest from the crowd.

"You may not know," Leslie Downing went on, "that I own the largest business in the area. I would like it to go on record that the present arrangement of the streams that flow through the area suits me perfectly. Any deviation in the arrangement will be detrimental. Changes in the system would prove expensive to me; coping with them would mean a costly and annoying disruption of life at Barnhouse. Therefore, I am prepared to sue all of you, including the town of Hamilton, to recoup the costs, real and emotional, that any scheme of yours entails. I'd like to put a question to the town: Are you prepared to bankrupt yourselves?"

Leslie Downing resumed her seat. There was an awkward momentary silence, and then a voice called out, "Hear, hear!" In an instant the enthusiasm caught, and most of the audience was on its feet, applauding loudly.

The scales had tipped, and now the preservation ladies began to talk at once. With great effort George Farnham managed to regain control of the proceedings. Some desultory give-and-take followed, but it was evident that the developers had given very little thought to the water issue. Elizabeth Bennet began to tell the property owners, in a thin and earnest voice, that the details would work themselves out; but she was quickly shouted down. Leslie Downing's question had effectively brought the town's galloping dream of sudden riches to a screeching halt. The preservation ladies swarmed around her, shaking her firmly by the hand, offering her pamphlets, and congratulating each other, one and all, on a hard-fought and well-deserved victory.

As Dewey made her way out through the crowd, she caught sight of the solitary figure of Leslie Downing, striding gracefully away. A remarkable woman, thought Dewey, as she waited at the main door for George Farnham. She wondered if the promised wrath of Leslie Downing would really be enough to make the developers turn tail.

George Farnham approached. "I knew it would come down to money, my dear," he said with a smile. "I think there will be little doubt on the matter when the council votes. Nobody wants to land us all in a lawsuit."

"George. You're so wise. Lucky for all of us that the money happened to be on the right side." She looked around as the Aviance representatives walked away toward their car. Dewey and George stood watching them.

"I wonder if they feel badly about it?" said Dewey.

"There are plenty of other lambs for the slaughter," responded George.

"Yes," said Dewey. "It's astounding how meekly they await the pleasure of the evening wolves."

25

EARLY THE NEXT morning, Willy Grimes appeared as usual to feed Midnight Blue. Dewey took one look at him and knew the boy was troubled.

"What's wrong, Willy?" she asked, opening Starbuck's stall door and leading the mare out into the sunlight to graze.

"It's not fair, Mrs. James, that Midnight has to stay in his stall all the time. It's like a prison. Look at him."

Midnight did indeed present a rather wistful appearance for a horse. Dewey was filled with sympathy. "I know, Willy. But please remember, my friend, to consider the alternative. I'm afraid Midnight is still enjoying the probation of the authorities. He has not been granted an official pardon."

"He'll probably never get out, now," said Willy sadly, stroking the stallion's neck. "Unless I spring him."

"You mustn't spring him, Willy." Dewey rubbed Midnight's nose gently. "He's bearing up. I'm sure we'll hear from Hugh shortly."

"I don't think so, Mrs. James."

"Why do you say that?"

"Oh, he's being weird. I think something's wrong with Hugh. I went to see him yesterday after school, and Scott Bauman told me to go away."

"Perhaps Hugh was busy. In a meeting with Mrs. Downing or something." Dewey tried to force conviction into her voice.

"No. He was at home." Willy's eyes filled with tears. "Mrs. James, I don't think they want me at Barnhouse anymore. I think Hugh's gonna fire me."

"Oh, Willy, no." She rubbed the top of Willy's head thoughtfully. Suddenly the boy began to cry in earnest.

"And I worked so *hard*," he said between sobs. "I did a really good job, Mrs. James, I did! I did!" Dewey folded her arms gently around him and listened as he poured out his unhappiness. When his sobs began to die down, she looked at him carefully.

"Willy," she said, "you must trust me. Come here, sit down." She took a seat on a bale of hay and pulled Willy down next to her. "I think Hugh must have something else on his mind."

"They wanna fire me!" he sobbed again.

"Hush, Willy, hush. No, I am quite certain you are wrong about that." She smoothed his limp hair up off his forehead and looked earnestly into his eyes. "I will get to the bottom of this for you, I promise."

"You can't do that," said Willy, full of miserable doubt.

"Oh, I think I can." She smiled. "And I think, Willy, that before too long the suspense will be over. For you and for Midnight. Please—trust me." She stood up and adopted a cheerful tone. "And, in the meantime, there is a great deal that needs doing around here. I need a handyman about the place. Do you think you can mend a fence for me, Willy?"

"Sure, Mrs. James." Willy had the look of one who is trying to forget his own unhappiness for the sake of a friend.

"I will pay you. It will be kind of like a business deal, but between friends."

"It will be exactly like a business deal," said Willy, flashing his deal-maker's smile.

They retired to the kitchen and drew up a work schedule for the next two weeks, which would bring them up to the close of school. After that, Dewey reasoned, Willy would resume his job at Barnhouse. She hoped.

Dewey finally sent Willy off to school, but he was bound to be late, she knew. With a glint of mischief in her eye, she concocted a note for the teacher, inventing on the spur of the moment an extra-credit project in library science.

Willy's face was a picture of dismay as he read the note

through. "Do I really have to do this, Mrs. James? It sure sounds boring."

"I'll help you with it, Willy, if worst comes to worst," she said, and sent him off on his bicycle.

Having cheered Willy Grimes, Dewey was left in the kitchen with her own uneasiness. "Isaiah," she remarked to her dog, "I think it's time for action." Isaiah lifted his head to regard her through sleepy eyes, wagging his tail in a slow, half-expectant rhythm. "Come on, boy. Once more into the breach." The tail wagged in earnest now as Isaiah stood and rushed to the door. Dewey opened it for him, and they climbed into the old station wagon.

Dewey wasn't sure what to expect from this visit to Hugh Shields, but she knew she had to confront him. She left Isaiah in the car and asked one of the grooms to direct her to Hugh's cottage.

Dewey knocked tentatively at the door.

"Come in," Hugh called.

Dewey opened the door and poked her head in. "Hugh?" She entered and looked about her. There were packing boxes scattered around, most half-full, containing a variety of odds and ends—books, trophies, photographs. On the couch was a big duffel bag, full. Shields had his back to the door; he was removing a large, framed photograph from the living room wall. "Hugh, it's me. Dewey."

He turned around to face her. "Hello, Dewey." In his arms was a photograph of a young Hugh Shields, with Leslie Downing and a jockey. In the background stood a beautiful stallion, with a blanket of flowers on his neck.

"Hugh, I need to talk to you. If you're not terribly busy." She cast an inquiring glance at the disarray in the small office.

"Come on in." Shields put down the picture and cleared a pile of papers from one of the chairs. "Welcome. Have a seat." His tone was flat and cool. Dewey had never known him to sound so distant. She sat, folding her hands primly in her lap.

"You mustn't run away."

He cleared off a corner of the sofa for himself and perched gingerly. "Don't now what you mean."

"Well," said Dewey, "correct me if I'm wrong. It looks to me as though you were packing."

"Thought maybe it was time to think of moving on."

"Any particular reason for going, just now?"

"No." Shields sighed. "Look, Dewey. This place is just getting to me. I'm getting old. Time to admit it and go."

"Oh, Hugh," Dewey's tone was sympathetic. "Things really are not as black as they seem. Won't you even discuss it?"

"Discuss what, Dewey?" He was clearly not going to help her. She let out a frustrated sigh.

"Well, there is of course a chance that I am wrong about this. I thought there was something you'd like to get off your chest. If I'm wrong, just say so." She waited, but he did not respond. "You have put up a remarkably good fight. I admire your strength in adversity." She paused, feeling her way. "It must have been terribly difficult for you, with that man taking over here. He couldn't hold a candle to you, and you knew it."

Shields looked away. "All water under the bridge, Dewey."

"You needn't mumble or make excuses to me. Considering everything, your behavior was completely understandable. Donald Irish must have been a singularly provoking man."

"You're right about that."

"A weaker man than yourself might have been more prompt to retaliate."

"I don't know what you mean."

Dewey shifted tactics. "You know, Hugh, I thought it was most peculiar when I heard about it. And then I got to thinking. Because Barnhouse has always been tremendously well run. Even an outsider like myself knows that. So it was mysterious." She paused to gauge her effect, but Shields's face was unreadable.

"You know, Hugh, that strange sequence of little events. Buttercups in the feed. A shredded girth. Valuable fillies out of place. All kinds of little misdemeanors. These struck me—and I daresay they struck Donald Irish—as the kinds of things a boy might get up to. A boy like Willy Grimes."

"Willy's no troublemaker."

"No. Certainly he is not. He has helped me admirably in the last week. He puts me to shame, he positively does. Everything in its place and so forth. He obviously cares deeply for his job."

Shields nodded. "He'll be the best trainer in the country if he keeps it up."

"That was the impression I had. His little corner of Barnhouse is a miracle of organization. He runs a tight ship. Like you do. Maybe you're his hero, Hugh."

Shields rubbed his eyes tiredly. "I'm nobody's hero, Dewey."

"And yet Donald Irish seemed to think Willy was behind the mischief at Barnhouse."

"Willy didn't do those things."

"I know that." Dewey waited.

"It was stupid of me." Shields said finally. He looked at Dewey, and his face was suddenly lined with pain and shame. "It was terrible. Someone might have been hurt."

"Tell me about it."

Shields regarded the boxes around him in a daze. "I guess I thought it had all gone far enough. I didn't like having Irish around. He was a bad influence on us all. Barnhouse wasn't the same, since he came. I wanted him out."

"Yes. One could hardly blame you."

Shields gave Dewey a look of disbelief; then he took up his story again.

"I had an idea. You see, Leslie took to putting him in charge of things when she went away. As if I wasn't here. So I thought I'd teach them both a lesson."

"So you played little tricks on people. Hoping that Irish's bad management or ignorance would be blamed."

"Yes. I thought that if Leslie got to hear about it, she'd realize that the man doesn't know horses. He knows numbers. Period. Good at numbers, he is. Was."

"And she would realize her mistake," said Dewey gently, "and so restore things to their proper order."

"That's right." Shields bent his head in shame.

"Poor Hugh," said Dewey. "You must have known it wouldn't work."

He looked up and stared off into space for a long moment. "No, it didn't work. Irish made sure that Leslie never heard about any of the little problems that came up while he was in charge. He fixed it all up, dealt with the tradesmen, argued with the grooms or the mechanics, with whoever. And whenever she came home, everything was in apple-pie order." His tone was bitter.

"Poor Hugh," Dewey said again, regarding him thoughtfully. "I imagine it felt like the end for you here."

"Well, that was pretty obvious, wasn't it?" He rose and began to pace the small sitting room in long, angry strides. "Here's old Hugh, doing things the same way as always. Only we're losing money. Going down the drain. Then *he* comes along and fixes it all. Fixes it!" Shields turned and glared angrily at Dewey. "Some damn-fool accountant in pinstripes comes in and sits down at an Italian desk. And suddenly I'm old-fashioned. Christ!"

Dewey nodded sadly. "It was you, wasn't it, that let Starbuck out of her stall?"

Shields sat down again suddenly, hiding his face in his hands. "Sorry about that, Dewey."

"Let me see if I can guess what you had in mind." She looked at him carefully. "A substitution, perhaps? At night?"

Shields nodded, looking glum. "I thought I'd take Midnight Blue out and hide him somewhere, or just leave him out for the night. Then I'd put your old mare in Midnight's box, so that there would be enough horses when the stable hands made the final count."

"And in the morning, when Leslie came down to the stables, there would be old Starbuck. An acknowledged beauty, but past her prime." Dewey laughed suddenly. "I'd have liked to have seen the look on Leslie Downing's face when that bit of alchemy was achieved." She threw Shields a mischievous look, but he was oblivious. He leaned with his arms on his knees, looking sadly at the floor.

"I know this has been dreadfully difficult for you, Hugh," she went on. "But you can't run away, not now. Barnhouse needs you more than ever."

"I'm going away, Dewey. I don't belong here anymore. Don't know just who does. This place has changed." He looked at her. "There's something I'd like you to do for me."

He rose and went to a small corner cupboard, returning with something in his hand. "This is for Willy. Will you give it to him for me?"

"What is it, Hugh?"

"Midnight's racing blanket. I wanted Willy to have it."

"Ah yes. The souvenir thing." Dewey took the blanket from him and stood up, unfolding the big red square and holding it out before her. "My, it's beautiful, isn't it? He'll be so pleased." Even in the dim light of the little cottage, the glorious blanket shone like a blaze of sunlight. "I do wish you'd reconsider, Hugh. This won't solve anything." She put a hand on his arm. "And it will break Willy's heart."

There was a knock at the door. As Dewey and Shields turned, Fielding Booker appeared in the doorway.

"Good morning, Dewey. Hugh."

"Hello, Bookie," said Dewey. Something in Booker's attitude made her uneasy. "I was just having a chat with Hugh," she gabbled. "We were talking about young Willy Grimes. The boy has a very bright future."

Booker paid no attention to Dewey's chatter. He had removed his hat and now stood somberly surveying the upheaval in the living room. "Hugh." He looked at the farm manager. "You'd better go, Dewey."

Dewey sat down firmly.

Booker looked at Shields again. "Hugh, I'm afraid I'll have to ask you to come with me."

"What in heaven's name do you mean, Bookie?" Dewey's tone was indignant.

"I am here on a painful duty, Hugh," said Booker, ignoring Dewey. "I'll need you to come with me."

Shields stared at Booker, his face full of resignation. Dewey bristled.

"Fielding Booker, I require you to answer me," said Dewey sternly, rising. "What on earth are you talking about?"

"Murder," said Booker sadly. "Murder. Hugh?"

Without a word, Hugh Shields pulled on his jacket and headed out the door. Booker started to follow, then caught sight of Dewey, who was still clutching the horse blanket.

"I'm afraid I'll need that, Dewey," he said, gently prising the blanket from her grasp. "Evidence. I'm sorry."

He turned and departed. Dewey looked about the room, where Hugh's belongings lay scattered in sad and silent little piles. Then she sat down hard on the sofa, deep in thought.

26

WITH RESPECT TO the recent events at Barnhouse, the little town of Hamilton was undergoing a change of heart. Its citizens had been, to a man, dry-eyed when they learned of the surprising manner in which Donald Irish had departed this earth. Nor had they grieved perceptibly when the awesome finger of justice had seemed to point to Peter Downing. Indeed, an inquiry into the truth of the matter would have shown that both of those circumstances had aroused a frisson of ghoulish enjoyment in Hamiltonians of every stripe.

This new situation, however, struck at the very soul of the town. Eyebrows were not raised; tongues did not wag. In the barrooms and the backyards where the matter was discussed, no snickers were heard. Hugh Shields was important to Hamiltonians; he was one of them. Tonight, as the news of his arrest made the rounds, the good watchers of Hamilton were afraid—for him, and for themselves. Most especially, for themselves.

As soon as Dewey had recovered from the shock of seeing Hugh arrested, she had rushed home to telephone George Farnham. They had gone together to the police station late in the day to talk to Booker, to learn what they could of the case against their friend. Fielding Booker, visibly shaken by the affair, had been reluctant to discuss it with them. He was clearly in low spirits himself, but he had finally laid the unwelcome facts before them. The sad little group sat together for an hour or more in Booker's office, as he recounted to Dewey and George the main points of the case.

"What about a lawyer for Hugh, Bookie?" George asked.

"I've spoken to Tony Zimmerman. He's seen Hugh and agreed to represent him. He's a good man."

"The best," agreed George.

"The best may not be good enough, George," Booker responded glumly.

The evidence, it appeared, had been mounting for days, and in the end Booker had been unable to ignore it. The fence post, which had cracked the banker's balding skull, was believed to have come from a pile of worn fence posts removed during the repairs. The repairs were under Shields's sole supervision, and no other members of the Barnhouse staff had touched them. According to one of the grooms, Shields had even gone so far as to prohibit the staff members from going near the fences under repair.

"When was this, Bookie?" Farnham asked wearily.

"Friday," the policeman replied in a tired voice. "The day of the murder."

"Oh, good heavens," Dewey exclaimed sadly. "But Bookie, that's hardly evidence."

"I know how you feel, Dewey," Booker replied, "but there is more. Much more."

He related to them the odd inconsistencies concerning Hugh's movements on the night of the murder. Peter Downing had called at the house; his claim that Shields had been asleep was of course unverified, and Shields had admitted to taking a "breath of air." Booker felt that, under oath, Downing would be forced to reveal that he had knocked at Hugh's door and had no reply.

"Wake Duncan with thy knocking," said Dewey, deep in thought. "What of it, Bookie? It seems to me that there was a great taking of walks that night. Hugh might have been checking on the horses."

"Then why not admit it?" Booker shook his head. "That would have been simple."

There was more to come. The most damning evidence of all, Booker informed them, was the evidence of the blanket. A preliminary exam at the forensic laboratory had revealed that the blanket did indeed hold clues to the grisly last moments of that indifferent banker's life.

Booker was grim. "We asked Hugh to search for that blanket; and he told Mike Fenton that he had. He told Mike that it could not be found." He looked at them both with an empty stare. "We found traces of what looks to be blood, and small perforations in the blanket. I believe the lab's report will confirm to us that the perforations were made by Irish's teeth, as he fought against suffocation."

Dewey brightened. "Bookie, I saw that blanket today. I held it up and looked at it. There were no bloodstains!"

"It may have been washed. But the lab tests will show them. Trust me, Dewey." He shook his head. "Sometimes I wonder why I ever got involved in police work. It would be easier, at times like these, to have found a different calling."

Dewey threw a glance in George's direction.

Booker continued with his tale. The motive, he informed them regretfully, was felt to be very strong. It had been obvious to him from the start, in fact. Donald Irish had been chipping away, day after day, at the rock of Shields's tenure at Barnhouse. Shields had found the situation intolerable, and he had finally cracked under the pressure.

The sad series of pranks, which Willy had related, had not stymied Booker for long. He had long suspected that Shields was the culprit. His impression was confirmed this afternoon, during the course of a long interrogation. Dewey nodded to herself sadly as the policeman recounted Shields's pitiful attempt to reassert himself at Barnhouse.

"You see, Dewey, I'm afraid that Hugh lost his perspective. He was losing his grip. For him to do such things, Dewey— that's not the Hugh Shields that we all thought we knew. It's terrible, I agree. But there it is. I'm afraid that we've got our man."

"But Bookie, it was surely not enough to prompt him to murder."

Booker disagreed. "He was on the point, Dewey, of losing everything to a smooth manipulator. His life's work was going down the drain, before his very eyes. Obviously, he couldn't take it any longer. I've seen this kind of thing before."

George Farnham spoke up. "I think we have to face it,

Dewey dear," he said, taking her hand gently. "Bookie doesn't like this any more than we do."

"And we have reason to believe that Mark Gordon was in league with Irish over a race-fixing scheme."

"Yes," said Dewey, "I felt sure there was something in it like that."

"You did?" Booker was surprised.

"Oh, yes," said Dewey. "I had a little chat with Peter Downing. He is thoroughly charming, and almost likable, you know. But not quite." She shook her head.

"Well, then, you can see what we're up against here. Hugh knew about the plans to fix the races, and was determined to put an end to Irish's influence at Barnhouse."

"That man was an interfering nitwit!" George exclaimed. Booker smiled for the first time all day.

"Peter Downing called him a sordid little idiot bean-counter," said Booker.

"Peter has always had a way with words," agreed Dewey. They fell silent. The huge clock on the wall ticked noisily.

"I hope," said Booker at last, "that we can make it manslaughter. Now that is strictly among the three of us. The prosecutor may be willing to go along. And I'm sure Tony Zimmerman will do his utmost."

"Even so . . ." began George, then broke off.

"Yes, George, you're right," said Booker, almost in a whisper. "Even so, this will be the end of Hugh. I'm afraid there is nothing I can do for him."

At the close of this long afternoon, a grim but practical George Farnham had persuaded Dewey to come around to his place for supper. Now they sat at his clean-lined kitchen table; the sliding doors that opened on to the river were open, letting in the fresh air of the summer evening. The sound of the water lapping gently against the banks reached their ears, and over this came the noise of crickets, going about their night's business. Dewey was making a brave and ineffectual attempt to eat an omelet George had prepared for them.

"You haven't touched your dinner, my dear. I'm afraid this

has been too much for you." George gave her a look full of grave concern.

"I'm sorry, George." Dewey poked at the food on her plate and attempted a smile. "I'm sicklied o'er with the pale cast of thought."

"Dewey, you know that Bookie is very fond of Hugh. This has been damned difficult for him."

"I know." She shook her head and gathered her purple sweater close about her as a light breeze blew in from the river. "I just hope he isn't making a terrible mistake. Or, rather, I hope he *is*. What do you think of Booker's case, George?" She put down her fork and looked hard at her friend.

Farnham was uneasy. "It covers a great deal of ground, Dewey."

"Ah, yes. But is it enough?" She poked at her omelet again. "George, what would you say was the best—the most persuasive—motive to murder?"

"Love, probably."

"Do you see love's hand in Bookie's case against Hugh?"

"He loves his job."

"That's not the same thing."

"Maybe he loves Leslie Downing."

Dewey brooded over this possibility. "Bookie's evidence is circumstantial. It might be applied equally well to a dozen people."

"What about the blanket?"

"George, don't be an idiot. If Hugh had used that blanket to suffocate Irish, he would never have kept it."

"Not if he was thinking straight. But we don't know how unbalanced all of this may have made Hugh."

"Or, assuming that he was crazy enough to keep a murderous blanket, he would certainly not have given it to me."

"Good point." George was thoughtful.

"And why murder?"

"To get Irish out of the way."

"But George—a telephone call to the racing authorities would have put an end to any race-fixing scheme."

"Self-defense? Maybe Irish threatened to kill Hugh if he spoiled the plan."

"Absurd. We would not be in this pickle if it were

self-defense." She thought, for a moment. "Name another strong motivation for murder, George."

"Money."

"Yes. *Cui bono*." She looked at George carefully, and there was a glint of satisfaction in her eye. "He has a great deal to say, our Bookie. But not enough. There are more things in heaven and earth than are dreamed of in his philosophy."

George was interested. "Dewey, I declare you have an idea about all of this. Tell me all." He pushed his plate aside and leaned closer.

Dewey shook her head. "Not yet, George," she replied in brisk tones. "I may need your help, however."

"Anything, my dear, anything at all."

"Good." She rose. "I'm going home to think."

"Dewey, this could be a dangerous game. I don't want you running any risks. I want to keep an eye on you."

"Never fear, George. If you want me tomorrow, I expect you may find me at the library."

"The library?" George stood and cocked his head to one side.

"Yes. The mystery and suspense section, I imagine. Thank you for the supper." She departed.

27

DEWEY JAMES ROSE quite early the next morning, for she anticipated a very busy day. She had sat up late into the night, drinking tea in a cozy red armchair, with her feet resting on the back of the snoring Isaiah. Finally, well past midnight, an inspiration had reached her tired brain, and she had sent Isaiah off to his doghouse.

Having slept on her idea, Dewey was convinced that she might be on the right track. There were still some facts that she needed to be sure of, and there was a great deal of research to be done. But first, she must see Hugh Shields. She pulled on her purple sweater and headed out to do battle.

She arrived at the police station shortly before nine and found Fielding Booker in conference with Tony Zimmerman. Both men looked as though they hadn't slept. Zimmerman, a tall, good-looking man in his middle forties, had shed his usual military uprightness; he sat dispiritedly in Booker's small office, a yellow legal pad in his lap. Booker, looking more defeated than Dewey had ever known him, greeted her with wary cordiality.

"Dewey," he said, rising. "I'm surprised to see you out so early."

"Are you, Bookie? It's nearly nine o'clock." Dewey's tone was cool and firm. "Hello, Tony."

"Morning, Dewey," said Zimmerman.

"Tony, I'd like to speak to Hugh, if you don't mind."

"I'm afraid he won't welcome a visit, Dewey. Nothing personal, you understand."

"Yes. I understand. If you would please give him a note for me, however, I believe he'll spare me a moment. This is not a sympathy call." She withdrew a note pad from her handbag and, perching on a chair, scribbled out a few lines. Then she carefully folded the paper over. "I hope he can read that. My writing is hopeless." She handed the note to Tony Zimmerman and sat back in her chair.

"I'm forgetting my manners, I'm afraid," said Booker. "Coffee, Dewey?"

"Yes, thank you, Bookie." A look of relief crossed Booker's face as he left the office to go in search of coffee.

"Fenton!"

He doesn't want to be trapped in here with a sexagenarian megalomaniac, thought Dewey, as Booker's voice rang out down the hall.

"Yes sir."

"Coffee for Mrs. James, if you please," Dewey heard him say in loud tones. There followed a murmured exchange that she hadn't a prayer of overhearing. The clock on the wall ticked loudly, and Dewey waited. Sergeant Fenton arrived and placed a cup on a small round table at her elbow; he was followed by Tony Zimmerman, who reappeared with a look of curiosity on his face.

"He asks please if you can wait till he's had a chance to freshen up. Won't be a minute."

Zimmerman sat down heavily and let out a sigh. "I don't mind telling you, Dewey, that this looks bad to me."

"You can't possibly believe that Hugh Shields is a murderer, Tony," said Dewey in reproving tones.

"Not important what I believe. First rule of criminal practice is, Don't ask the guy if he's guilty." He scratched his cheek. "The problem is, can the state prove it?"

"I've heard all of that before, thank you, Tony, and don't need your eyewash this morning." She looked at him sternly and took a swallow of coffee.

A young police officer appeared in the doorway and cleared his throat. "If you'll follow me, Mrs. James?" Dewey set down her coffee cup and followed the young man through the large steel door at the end of the main corridor. He showed her in to a small, cramped interview room that was fitted out with two metal chairs and a tiny wooden table. As Dewey sat down, the officer spoke.

"I'm afraid I'll have to ask you to leave that with me, Mrs. James," he said, indicating her handbag.

"That's quite all right, Officer. You're Tim Cleary, aren't you?"

"Yes, ma'am."

"Yes, well, Officer Cleary. The weapons are concealed about my person, so here you go." She handed him the purse and watched with some amusement as the young policeman felt his way through her small jest. Finally a smile broke out on his face.

"Just a minute, ma'am." He disappeared and, a moment later, returned with Hugh Shields. Cleary retreated to the regulation distance from them, positioning himself just outside the open door to the small room.

Leslie Downing's right-hand man seemed to have shrunk overnight. He still wore the jeans and the blue work shirt that Dewey had seen him in yesterday, but his clothes hung limply on his frame. All the spring was gone from his step, and there was a glazed look in his tired eyes. He sat down wearily at the table, looking almost without interest at Dewey.

"Forgive me for intruding on you like this, Hugh, but I thought it might be important. I hope you don't mind."

Her graciousness put him momentarily at ease.

"No bother, Dewey. I'm at home to you any day." His tone was less bitter than his words. Dewey felt encouraged.

"I have given this situation a great deal of thought, Hugh, and there is something I need you to tell me." She held up her hand in admonishment as he began to speak. "The problem is, I'm not quite certain exactly what it is I need to know. If you follow me."

"So far." He nodded.

"Good. Now then. First of all, I want to know why you refused to talk to Willy Grimes the other day, when he came to see you." She sat back and waited for his reply.

"I don't know, Dewey. I think I was just feeling bad, in

general. About those stupid tricks I played. I didn't want to let him down."

Dewey shook her head vehemently. "No, Hugh. That won't do. You have been pulling those stunts for several weeks. And if you had really been worried about living up to Willy's ideal, your awkwardness in his presence would have revealed itself sooner. So that won't do."

Dewey waited. Shields met her silence with his own.

"Very well; never mind. I shall see, later, if my little assumption is correct." She leaned forward across the table, fixing him with a long, hard look. "Hugh, there was something on your mind when Peter Downing came to see you on Wednesday night. He thought you were unhappy. I think you were trying to puzzle something out."

Hugh nodded, surprised at her assessment. "Yes, Dewey, I was."

"Tell me, if you please."

Shields took a deep breath. "Something I found in Irish's desk. A notebook."

"You were going to ask him about it?"

"I don't know, exactly, what I was going to do." He paused. "I didn't think it was his, you see. And it would have been hard to confront him."

"Because you had no business rifling his desk."

"That's it."

"Describe it to me, Hugh, if you please."

"A little spiral job. You know, like kids use in school."

"Big? Small?"

"Little. Two by three, or so."

"What was in it, Hugh?"

"Just some notes that I couldn't really make much of. Hardly anything, really."

"What made you suspicious of it in the first place?"

"It was the way Irish locked it away. Careful. Real careful. And he didn't know that I had seen him do it. He looked around, then took it out of his pocket and put it way back in a file drawer but forgot to lock it."

"And you took it out again?"

"Not then. Not till later. I read it, out of curiosity. Or really, more than that. Because I figured he and Gordon were into something together. The way they pretended not to know each other."

Dewey was surprised at this. "Do you mean they did know each other?"

"No—not necessarily. I mean, I had no reason really to think so. But Gordon acted strange around him. Kind of formal. Fake. I thought it was an act."

"There's no art," said Dewey, "to find the mind's construction in the face." She thought for a moment. "Did you have any idea what they might be up to?"

"Fixing races, was my guess," said Hugh.

"I wonder if that was it. All right, then. You replaced the notebook in Donald Irish's desk. What happened next? Did you find anything out?"

"No. I didn't get a chance to ask him about it. Or maybe I didn't have the nerve."

"But it bothered you still?"

"I guess so. And a couple of days later, I thought about looking at it again."

"Friday?"

"Yes."

"And on Friday, you removed it from his desk?"

"Yes, I got it out of the desk to have a look. Then Irish turned up, kind of unexpected, and I thought the best thing would be to take it home with me. I could replace it the next morning."

"But then, of course, there was no need, the next morning."

"No."

"Hugh, where is the notebook now?"

"In my office."

"Where, exactly?"

"I taped it to the back of the calendar. Hanging on the wall behind the desk. Dewey, is this important?" For the first time this morning, Shields sounded interested.

"I'd like to take a look at it. Do I have your permission?"

Shields let out a resigned chuckle. "I think you'll have to ask the authorities, Dewey."

She rose. "I thank you, Hugh, for seeing me this morning. Try to stay in good heart."

Dewey stopped in at Booker's office. Zimmerman had left, and the policeman was just finishing a telephone call when she poked her head in at his door. "Bookie, I need to ask a favor of you."

"What's that, Dewey?"

"I would like to have permission to retrieve something from Hugh's office. You are welcome to come with me, if you like, or to send Sergeant Fenton."

"Why, thank you, Dewey, that's really magnanimous."

"Oh, Bookie, don't. Please. I have a busy day today, and I'm not in the mood for irony."

"Sorry. That was uncalled for. All right, Dewey, suppose you tell me what this thing is that you need. Sit down, please."

Dewey sat and described, briefly, her conversation with Shields. "I want to look at that notebook, Bookie. Please."

Booker stood and reached for his hat, which was lying on a folding chair. "I have no objection to your taking a look, Dewey. But I'd better come along. The very fact that Hugh concealed this book is a matter for us, you see."

"Yes, I know. I just want to read it, that's all."

"Without you, it might have taken us a long time to find it. So I think you have a right. Shall we?"

"Yes." Dewey reclaimed her handbag from Officer Cleary, and she and Booker headed out the door.

28

DEWEY AND BOOKER arrived together at the Barnhouse business office twenty minutes later. The little outbuilding had been sealed with yellow tape. When they entered, Dewey noticed that the place bore a melancholy air of neglect. It was like a theater the day after the show has closed, before the set has been struck.

The wall calendar hung behind Hugh's desk; it was still turned to the May page, and the lesser cloverleaf weevil gazed out at the intruders suspiciously. But they had no trouble finding the notebook.

Booker opened the little book. It was rather new, and nearly empty; but the last page held a few scribbled notes, written in a large hand with a ball-point pen. Booker adjusted his hat thoughtfully. *Ck co,* they read, and *security? s.p. list reit uccls.*

"Can't imagine what Hugh made of this, Dewey."

"He didn't know what to make of it, Bookie—but he thought it was strange that Irish had tucked it away so carefully. Now that I've seen it, I agree with him. It's very odd indeed." She furrowed her brow as she puzzled over the disjointed notes. "May I borrow it?"

Booker was reluctant. "This may be evidence. I don't see how I can let you have it."

"Well, then, Bookie, you must let me make a copy."

"Dewey, I think you should tell me what you're up to here. If you'll forgive my saying so, you're out of your depth. Let me spare you the trouble of trying to get to the bottom of a police matter. I can save you a great deal of time."

She shook her head. "You are a most thoughtful fellow, Bookie, a ver' parfit gentleman. But I would rather do this on my own."

He gave her a long look, sighed, and relented. "I'll take it round to the office and have a copy made for you."

"Thanks, Bookie. Mind if I tag along?" She smiled innocently.

"Dewey, I think you're getting in awfully deep. Your shenanigans are not going to help Hugh."

"Not as deep as some. Shall we go, Bookie? *Tempus fugit*."

"As you say, Dewey. Time does fly."

With her precious photocopy clutched tightly in her grasp, Dewey made her way from the police station to the library, where the members of the Calvert delegation to the literacy program were due to arrive at noon. She got there a few minutes before the hour and greeted Tom Campbell with a distracted air. Then she sat down to wait patiently at the front desk. She had an idea, but wanted an expert opinion. Alastair Keith, confidence man, was just the expert she needed.

At noon precisely the old glass door opened to admit Alastair Keith in the company of Nils Reichart and one other man. To Dewey's mind, the stranger had more of the appearance of a prisoner. He was young and rather heavyset; as the little party made its way into the library, he looked about him with an air of uncertainty, as if he had just disembarked after a long sea voyage. Dewey supposed he must feel disoriented by the cozy setting.

The group made its way to the desk. "Mrs. James, good morning to you," said Alastair Keith in hearty tones. "May I present Phil Danvers? Phil, this is Mrs. James, our patroness."

"Hi ya," said Phil Danvers, raising a hand in salute.

"Hello, Dewey," said Nils Reichart.

"Good morning to you all." Dewey beamed at Reichart. "This is a big day for the Hamilton library, Mr. Danvers. We are all tremendously pleased about the program. I hope you are, too?" She smiled cheerily and put her head on one side.

"Yeah," said Phil Danvers.

"Wonderful. Nils, I am hoping you'll have a little time for

us today. There is a young man due here in half an hour to see
Mr. Keith; and I believe Susan Miles is scheduled to work with
Mr. Danvers. Could you spare a moment to introduce Mr.
Danvers to Tom Campbell? He's in the staff room."

"Sure thing, Dewey." The two men headed toward the back,
and Dewey turned to speak to Alastair Keith.

"Mr. Keith, I have a little puzzle before me, and I would like
your help in solving it."

"Anything at all, Mrs. James. It will be my pleasure to assist
with whatever means I may have at my disposal."

"Good. Your particular expertise will fill the lacunae in my
education." Good heavens, thought Dewey to herself, his
oratory is catching. "Let's have a seat, then, shall we?" They
retired to the reference section and seated themselves once
more at the little table there.

"Mr. Keith, I believe you mentioned that the reason for
your—er—tenure at Calvert is that you perpetrated a fraud?"

"Perpetrated several, Mrs. James. I only had the misfortune
to be apprehended on one occasion. But yes. Not to put too fine
a point on it, you might say I cooked some books."

"Perfect," said Dewey with a smile. "Then I'm sure you'll
be able to help me out." Her tone became serious. "Perhaps
you have heard about the recent tragedy in Hamilton, Mr.
Keith?"

He nodded. "A murder. We have heard all about it."

"Yes. The police have made an arrest, but there is an—I
guess you might call it an *angle* that I should like to explore."

"The amateur sleuth?" Keith was amused.

"Oh, good heavens no. Just the town busybody. As everyone will tell you. They think me eccentric, and I'm quite sure
they're correct."

"A generally pleasing eccentricity, if I may so say, Mrs.
James," said Keith handsomely. Dewey fished in her handbag
for a piece of notepaper, studiously ignoring the man's appreciative gaze.

"My question for you, Mr. Keith, is this. Let us say you had
been given free rein to improve the financial picture of a failing
business. And in half a year, you had managed to turn the
whole thing around and make it profitable. Is there a way to do

such a thing, without actually doing it, if you catch my drift?"

Keith chuckled. "Hundreds of ways. Can you be more specific?"

"I'm afraid I can't, just at present. But let me fill you in. And I'll ask you, please, to take a look at this." Dewey opened up her photocopy of the strange notebook entry. Then she leaned closer and outlined, in quiet and serious tones, her idea.

"Yes," chuckled Keith, when he had heard Dewey's exposition. "Rather an interesting setup. And almost foolproof, unless it had been discovered."

Dewey nodded. "That's what I thought, Mr. Keith."

"You're quite a clever girl, if I may say so, Mrs. James." He smiled broadly.

Dewey blushed. This Alastair Keith really was a most disarming man. But years younger than herself. And a felon into the bargain. "The problem remains for me, Mr. Keith, of finding some kind of proof."

"Well, now, perhaps I can help you with that. At the very least, I can tell you where to look. Although I warn you that it may require some rather tedious research."

"I'm a librarian," said Dewey with a smile. "I was born to dig through musty files, and am rarely dismayed. If you'll tell me where you think is the most likely place to look, I shall approach this task with gusto."

"All right then. If I were you, I should pay a visit, first of all, to the county clerk's office. Here is what you'll be looking for." He gave Dewey a few details to aid her in her research, and then glanced at the clock on the wall. "Now, if you'll forgive me, Mrs. James, I think it's time for my appointment with my tutee."

"Oh, yes, please, Mr. Keith. I don't want to be in the way of Mr. Campbell's program. Forgive my taking up so much of your valuable time."

"Time is one commodity that I seem to have in abundance, Mrs. James," Keith replied gravely.

"Well, you have done us all a very good turn here today, Mr. Keith. I thank you." Dewey put away her notebook.

Keith rose. "Paying my debt to society. All in a day's work, where I come from." He gave her a shy and rather charming smile. "Do you know, I wish I'd met you sooner. I might have spared myself some of this, if I'd known the influence of a woman such as yourself." He bowed and strode gracefully to the front desk, the picture of educated elegance. The only jarring element was the huge black radio bracelet, locked firmly in place about his ankle.

29

THE OFFICES OF the county clerk occupied almost the entire second floor of the Grain Merchants' Exchange. The room was cavernous and depressing, fitted out with decidedly worn furnishings that must have dated from the New Deal. Ancient steel file cabinets, their surfaces aglow with the greasy dust of decades, lined three walls. Against the fourth was a library of oversized gray-green deed books; these held, between their imposing covers, the tortuous records of every recorded property transaction in Hamilton County over the course of two centuries. At the center of the room was a huge oak table bearing a microfilm machine that looked queerly out of place; next to it was an aged photocopier, whose mechanism was wont to creak in loud protest whenever anyone set it a task.

Dewey marched up to a long wooden counter that ran across the middle of the room. On the other side, seated at a gray steel desk, was a woman of uncertain years, her doughy face surmounted with a cloud of blue hair. A nameplate announced her as Miss Hilda Beane. She looked up reluctantly at Dewey's approach, and her scowl indicated plainly that she was in no mood for interruption.

"Good afternoon, Miss Beane," said Dewey.

"I'm very busy today. Can it wait?"

"No, I'm afraid not," said Dewey, noting the blue hair. This was one mystery solved, at least. Now she knew who used Doris Bock's special blue henna rinse.

"I'll be with you in a few minutes," said Miss Beane coldly, returning her abstracted gaze to a yellow form on her desk. The telephone began to ring. Miss Beane ignored it. Dewey counted twelve full rings; the thirteenth was more of a muffled death squeak.

Miss Beane stared at the paper, turned it over, and shook her head. With a loud sigh she reached for a rubber stamp, set it down on the document with a thump, and replaced the stamp carefully in a small metal rack. Then she examined the yellow form again, initialed it, and put it in a wire basket marked "Processing," atop a huge stack of similar-looking forms. Dewey wondered briefly to herself just how long the paper would be condemned to wait in the basket. I suppose my troubles don't amount to a Hilda Beane's, she thought inanely, and giggled aloud.

Miss Beane shot her a reproving look. "Yes?"

"Yes," said Dewey firmly. "I'd like to look at the Uniform Commercial Code statements."

Miss Beane sighed. "Over there." She flicked her eyes toward a group of files in a far corner of the room.

"Is there any special arrangement?"

"What do you mean?"

"That is to say," pursued Dewey, with increasing politeness, "perhaps you can tell me the best way to go about looking through them."

"You just look." Hilda Beane sighed again and rose reluctantly from her desk. "I'll show you." She pulled open a small drawer, about the size of a library card catalog file. "They're arranged alphabetically. See, here's ABC Contractors. Someone has filed a statement listing several of their trucks."

"I see." Dewey looked with dismay at the file cabinet. There were two dozen drawers. But if her hunch were right, she should be able to find what she was looking for in a few minutes. "Thank you very much, Miss Beane."

"Don't remove anything," said Miss Beane sternly as she returned to her desk. "If you remove anything, I will have to ask you to fill out a form."

Heaven preserve us, thought Dewey.

The phone began to ring again. Miss Beane picked up another yellow form from her in basket and began to sigh over it in earnest.

It took Dewey very little time to find what she was looking for. It was right there, under B for Barnhouse. The statement listed the goods against which a security interest was held. "Three thoroughbred racing horses, as follows. 'Meretricious'; 'Our Man Fritz'; 'Stanley Steamer'." Opposite the horses' names were their registration numbers. According to the statement, the creditor was a company called Questor, Inc.

Dewey thanked Hilda Beane and, deep in thought, went up two flights of stairs to George Farnham's office.

"Hello, George."

Farnham greeted Dewey with a warm smile. "Dewey. Come in, come in." He rose and went to the door, leading her in to take a seat. "Feeling a bit better today, my dear?"

"Yes, thank you, George. I have just been doing a little research. All thanks to a most educational conference with an engaging criminal."

"What on earth are you talking about?" George resumed his seat at the desk.

"A Mr. Keith, from the Calvert prison."

"Oh, the literacy program. Is he one of the participants?"

"Yes, in a way. It turns out that he is extremely well educated, and has volunteered his services as a tutor in our program. In exchange, he has offered to be a security guard at the library."

"Turnabout is fair play," said George. "That's an interesting twist. How is Tom Campbell taking it?"

Dewey laughed. "They are fast friends. Mr. Keith is unmatched, in Hamilton, for oratorical powers. And he has an English accent. So naturally he has quite captivated Tom."

"Oh, dear," chuckled George.

"Anyway, George, he has helped me quite a bit with my idea."

George looked alarmed. "Dewey, dear, you mustn't go recruiting criminals in a murder investigation."

"Oh, George, you sound like Tom Campbell." Farnham looked hurt. "You *do*, George. Don't pout. I consider your attitude unenlightened. Besides, he's not a murderer. He's a thief."

"Oh, well. In that case you did quite right."

"Don't be difficult, George. An embezzler and a confidence man, actually, you see. With quite a lot of experience in business."

"Dewey, be frank. Don't spare me. Perhaps Tom Campbell is not the only one who is captivated." Dewey shot him a look of rebuke. "Aha!" George exclaimed. "Well, well. I won't say a word."

"George, you are being absurd."

"Am I? Well. What sort of wisdom has this man of affairs provided you?"

"He has merely confirmed a suspicion that I had."

"Yes?"

"That Donald Irish's remarkable, miraculous success at Barnhouse may have been less substantial than everyone thought."

"I don't follow you."

"You will. George, I'd like some information about those people who came to the town meeting. Have you got it on hand?"

"You mean the Aviance Reality group? Of course. I have quite a file on them. What's it all about, Dewey?"

"Will you do a little research for me, George?"

"Anything, my dear."

"I want you to go carefully through the file on that company. You may have to look into the state records, as well."

"The company is a realty trust. A partnership. The actual ownership may be hard to trace."

"I want to know the names of the investors in the development scheme, George."

"I have them right here." He indicated a file cabinet against the wall.

"No, not the investors of record. I want to find out whose money was really behind that project. And I want you to find out about a company called Questor, Inc." She jotted down the name on a piece of paper on George's desk. "I think you'll find a relationship of some sort between the two."

"You think there's some connection with Irish's death?"

"In a way." She considered for a moment. "I have an errand to run, now. I'll phone you shortly. Thank you, George."

30

THIS TIME, FIELDING Booker abandoned any pretense at being glad to see Dewey James arrive. He was leaning back in his chair, with his feet up on his desk, when she presented herself once more at his office door. He greeted her with a wary nod, reluctantly lowering his feet to the ground.

"I know you think me an intrusive old busybody, Bookie, but I promise you this is important."

"*Au contraire*, Dewey." Booker looked at her impassively. "I'm beginning to think of you as a colleague. So you'll forgive my bad manners. All in the name of business."

"Please don't tease me, Bookie. You'll disrupt my train of thought."

"In that case, have a seat, Detective."

"Thank you. But I really can't stay. And neither can you."

"Oh, Dewey." Booker rubbed his eyes. "Where are we off to now?"

"We may need a subpoena. Can you get one?"

"For what?"

"Banking records."

"That depends. Sit down, Dewey. Please." She sat. "Now, begin at the beginning, please, and go on until you reach the end."

Dewey took a deep breath. "I think you should look into that loan to Barnhouse. I have just been to the office of the county clerk, where I found something quite astonishing."

"What—Hilda Beane going cheerfully about her job?"

"She was rather a tough nut," Dewey agreed. "Fortunately,

however, I knew, more or less, what to look for. Thanks to Mr. Keith."

"Ah, yes. Your light-fingered Londoner. The Calvert authorities had to take away his bumbershoot, although I hear he gets the *Financial Times* delivered to his cell. Nils Reichart thinks he's quite taken with you, Dewey."

"He has been enormously helpful. And I do think he wants to reform. But that's beside the point."

"Yes. So it is. Go on."

"Well now. We all thought that the reason Donald Irish had been able to turn Barnhouse around, financially, was that his bank had provided a loan. And then he himself had, quite naturally, taken an interest in the object of that loan. Lent a hand at Barnhouse. Took over the financial reins from Hugh."

"Yes, that's right."

"We had the idea in view that he was behaving like a responsible banker."

"Exactly. A zealous banker."

"Bookie, I don't think there was a loan."

"What? Dewey—"

"I think we shall discover as much. There was money, certainly, from somewhere. But no bank loan. Come on, Bookie. Let's go. If I'm wrong about this, I promise I will never bother you again. Never darken your door."

Booker's interest was aroused by this rash promise. With a sigh, and against his better instincts, he committed himself to pursuing Dewey James's crazy idea. "You win, Dewey." He stood and reached for his hat.

"Fenton!" he called. Sergeant Fenton appeared at the door. "Sir."

"Mikey. Lord help me. We're off to see Miss Mole."

"I'll have a hot bath waiting for you on your return, sir."

Marjorie Mole's office was somewhat less awful than her living room. There was no potpourri, for one thing, to choke you in a vicious stranglehold of fragrance. And because the offices had glass walls, there was sunlight. Unfortunately, however, there was still Miss Mole. No matter how you looked at the situation, there was no getting around that.

Dewey and Booker had been there for a full ten minutes, explaining the nature of the inquiry they wished to make. Now Booker was patiently explaining again.

"Miss Mole, I am not asking you to reveal the confidential information of your client records. In fact, I suggest that you will discover no such record. In which case, there can be no confidence to violate. Do you follow me?" He spoke slowly, as though issuing a command to a very backward dog.

Marjorie Mole giggled and pushed a lank strand of damp-looking hair up off her forehead. She extended one fleshy pink hand toward a small jar on her desk, opened it, and extracted a small purplish lump. "Pastille?"

"No, thank you, Miss Mole." Booker glowered at her as she popped the horrid lump into her dreadful mouth.

"Miss Mole—" Dewey began.

"Are you with the police?" Snicker.

"Yes, she is," said Booker firmly. "I have deputized Mrs. James for the purpose of this examination. She has a badge in her handbag. Miss Mole, I would like your cooperation."

"I don't see how I can help you, Captain." Titter. "I really don't."

Outside on the main banking floor, the customers and tellers were beginning to look toward the office with curious glances.

"Miss Mole, I am prepared to make life extremely difficult for you. Beginning now!" Booker slammed his palm hard on her desk. The candy jar shook. Marjories Mole grew pale, and her eyes filled with tears. Dewey glared disapprovingly at Booker, but there was a look of patient satisfaction on his face. Dewey waited, curious, as Marjorie Mole withdrew a handkerchief from her sleeve. She dried her eyes and blew her nose discreetly, then smiled weakly at Booker.

"I'm sorry, Captain. It's all been so difficult for me." She sniffled. "Tell me exactly what you want to know. I'm sure I'll do everything I can to help."

"Thank you, Miss Mole. I would like for you to examine the loan records for the last six months, and just let me know the file number of a business loan made to Barnhouse Stables. I don't need to know anything else. The terms you may keep as dark as you like. I just want to know if it was made."

"I believe it was October," put in Dewey. Booker looked at her inquiringly. "Gossip," she said, winking at him.

Marjorie Mole rose with a sniffle and walked sturdily out onto the main banking floor, heading for a rank of beige file cabinets. Booker watched her go with distaste. "Lord, how I detest that woman," he muttered. Dewey nodded in sympathy.

Miss Mole returned in five minutes with a puzzled look on her face. "I can't find the file," she said.

"Do you mean that the file is missing, Miss Mole?" Booker asked. She responded with a blank look.

Dewey interposed. "Miss Mole, our professions are somewhat allied. That is to say—" she hesitated as Marjorie Mole turned her beady eyes to meet her gaze "—that is, we both rely on a systematic keeping of records. Mine, as you no doubt are aware, is the Dewey Decimal System. Antiquated but functional, like myself. In the library system, everything is assigned a number. But the system is not exactly sequential. There can be potential numbers. You might call them gaps. We must have these gaps, in fact; so that you can build your collection without having to renumber everything."

Booker stirred restlessly in his chair. "Let me handle this," he said under his breath. Dewey ignored him and went bravely on.

"Your system, however, would probably be sequential. You would assign the next number in the series, no matter what kind of loan it is. Am I right?"

Marjorie Mole giggled. "Yes, that's right." She reached for another purple candy. Booker looked at Dewey appreciatively.

"Miss Mole," he said, in gentle but firm tones, "is there a gap?"

"No. No gap."

"All the numbers in that sequence have files assigned to them?"

"Yes."

"And the files are there?"

"Yes." She rolled the candy around in her mouth. "All present and accounted for." She tittered.

"So when you say that you cannot find a file corresponding

to a loan to Barnhouse Stables, you mean that no such file exists," Booker persisted.

"Well, it can't, can it? There's no gap. Like she said." Marjorie Mole nodded toward Dewey.

"No gap. No file. No record of any loan from the Warren State Savings and Loan to Barnhouse Stables."

"That's right." She retrieved her awful handkerchief and blew her nose once more. "Pastille?" she giggled.

Dewey and Booker fled.

31

WHEN THEY REGAINED the fresh air outside the bank, Dewey and Booker paused for breath on the sidewalk.

"Oh, my, what a difficult interview," said Dewey.

"Dewey, I congratulate you. I thought I was the only person who knew how to get through to her. Now I think you had better let me take things from here."

"You were marvelous, Bookie. She is really quite something. Do you know, I feel as though I'd like to wash my hands."

"Yes, she has that effect." He looked seriously at Dewey. "Dewey, once again I thank you. But now it's time for you to return to your own concerns. I'll let you know if this leads to anything that will help Hugh. But I warn you—" he looked kindly at Dewey "—not to get your hopes up. In my experience—"

"You're absolutely right, Bookie. You just let me know." Dewey looked at him meekly. Booker was filled with distrust.

"What are you up to now?"

"Good-bye, Bookie!" Dewey began to head off down the street.

"Now, just wait a minute, Dewey." She paused and looked back at him. "If you are up to something, it's your duty to ask for my approval."

"May I go and see George, Bookie?"

"I think I'd better come along."

"The more the merrier." She strode briskly away.

"Dewey, I warn you, if this is some cockamamy scheme—"

"Come *on*, Bookie!"

They headed down Howard Street toward the Grain Merchants' Exchange. As they walked, Booker pressed her for information. Finally, Dewey gave in and told Booker about the document she had found earlier in the day.

"I was convinced there was some kind of fiddle going on. Because the Uniform Commercial Code statement was filed last fall, right about the time that Irish was supposed to have arranged for the loan from the bank."

"And this document does what, exactly, Dewey?"

"According to Mr. Keith, it indicates a security interest in property. In case of bankruptcy, the holder of the security interest is guaranteed to receive the items listed, regardless of the claims of other creditors. In this case, those beautiful horses. But you see, it wasn't filed by the bank. So there was no loan from the bank. Which means, of course, that there was something afoot."

"Well, not necessarily. Irish could have arranged the loan on his own. It would have been perfectly legal. You're a bright gal, Dewey, but you had best leave this kind of thing to the lawyers."

Dewey ignored the sermon. "If it was legal, why pretend it came from the bank?"

"Hmm." They reached the Grain Merchants' Exchange and began the long climb up to George Farnham's fourth-floor office.

"I think, Bookie," she remarked as they went up, "that Donald Irish raised money from somewhere else."

"I don't see how it matters. He raised the money," puffed Booker, rendered breathless by the climb "—and Barnhouse is fine, as a result."

"Is it?" They reached the fourth floor and headed down the hall, between the long rank of oak doors, to George Farnham's office.

"Well, yes. We know that."

"But we don't. In fact, we don't know anything at all about it, really. We only believe what we've been told." She gave him a piercing look as they knocked at George's office door.

George Farnham had about him an air of suppressed

excitement. He waited patiently as Dewey and Booker seated themselves and briefly recounted their interview with Marjorie Mole.

"I commend you for your bravery in facing the Mole woman, Bookie," said George. "She's awful. Eats those dreadful purple candies while she does business with you, and laughs at everything you say."

Booker shuddered. "She makes my flesh crawl, I don't mind telling you, George."

"You're too hard on her," put in Dewey, with an attempt at sincerity. "She's probably miserably unhappy."

"She deserves to be," replied Booker.

"Bookie, you're horrid." Dewey turned to George. "What news, Horatio?"

"Your crystal ball is in working order, my dear."

"I *knew* it!"

"What's all this?" Booker asked. Dewey filled him in quickly on the job she had given George. "I thought there must be a connection, you see, between the organization which had the security interest in Barnhouse, and the people who wanted to buy up all that property."

"Sinister," said Booker. "I don't like it."

"No," agreed Dewey.

"There's more," said George. "There's something even you didn't predict, Dewey. Let me show you this. I think you'll agree that it's interesting." He produced a huge expanding file, crammed full of papers. "Although I admit it doesn't look it. Now. Here we are."

He handed them a fat file folder. "Those are documents relating to the ownership of the Aviance Realty Trust. You know the kind of outfit it is. Where you can put a certain amount of money in and get about ten times as much back. Just while you sit there. Lawyers do all the work for you, buy the properties, oversee their development, and sell them."

"Yes, I know the kind of thing."

"You missed the town meeting, I think, Bookie. But you must have heard about the bloody battle we had. About the development of that huge chunk of land north of town, running between the river and Adams Hill."

"South of Barnhouse, then."

"To the south of it, and the north of it."

"I see," said Booker with interest. He looked through the papers in the folder quickly. "And?"

"And. This. The firm that represents Aviance is Baker, Ledyard and Dixon. Their office is in Chicago."

"Go on, George, the suspense is killing us," said Dewey impatiently.

Booker looked at his friend.

"That's young Peter Downing's firm," said George with a satisfied smile.

Booker made haste to pick up Peter Downing. Clearly the young lawyer knew a great deal more about the business than he had told them. "I knew he was a rascal," Booker said before he left them. "He probably thought we'd never turn up the connection. He's done for now. I'm just glad I asked him to stay in town for a few days."

When Booker was gone, George smiled broadly at Dewey. "It looks like old Hugh is off the hook, eh, my dear?"

"Oh, yes, George. I never had any doubt that Hugh was innocent of murder."

"Bookie didn't see it that way. I guess he's got his man now, though. He should be able to handle it all from here."

"You think so?"

"Of course. Come on, my sweet. We'll sup."

Dewey looked alarmed. She wished George would give up on the romantic angle.

"What's the matter?" George gazed at her soulfully. "Are you pining for your handsome felon, Dewey?"

"Oh, George, stop."

"Oh, I can see the lay of the land now. Well, my dear, if I'm bested, I'm bested. I can't compete with a bowler-hatted embezzler. Not if he's won your fair heart."

Dewey giggled. "Where shall we go, George?"

"The best place in town. *Chez moi.*" He gathered a few things into his briefcase, and they headed out the door. "We'll shop first, if you don't mind," he remarked, pausing to lock the office door. He smiled at Dewey. "With this same key,

Shakespeare unlocked his heart," he pronounced, turning the key in the door.

"If so, the less Shakespeare he!" retorted Dewey, with a laugh. George smiled and gave her his arm, and they headed down the stairs.

George Farnham was feeling particularly pleased with himself. In consequence, he made for Dewey a stupendous dinner of Cajun popcorn and blackened redfish. The kitchen was a disaster, but George was delighted. They sat in the candlelit dining room, drinking red wine in companionable silence and listening to the sounds of the summer twilight.

"I wonder how Bookie fared with young Peter Downing," George remarked at last.

"He won't get very far with him, I'm afraid," said Dewey.

"I expect he knows how to cover himself. But it was a terrible thing for him to do, letting Hugh be accused of the crime."

"I don't suppose he could help it," said Dewey.

"Come on, Dewey, it's time you gave up being a champion for that scamp."

She gave him a look of pitiful concern. "George."

"Yes, my dear."

"It's getting late."

"Dewey, it's only a quarter to eight."

"And we have an early day tomorrow."

"We do?"

"Yes. I'll need you at my place by seven-thirty."

George looked mystified. "Whatever for?"

"I'll tell you tomorrow. Will you be there?"

"You know I will."

"Thank you. And thank you for the dinner. I must get home and see to poor old Isaiah. He probably thinks I don't love him anymore."

"He probably thinks you've thrown him over for an English setter with dubious papers," remarked George, with a sad smile.

32

DEWEY HADN'T SLEPT well. One thing remained to be done, and she was not looking forward to it. She had formulated a plan to carry out this difficult task, but it left her feeling nervous and sick at heart. She was very glad when Willy Grimes turned up shortly before six-thirty.

"Hi ya, Mrs. James," said Willy cheerfully.

"Good morning, Willy." Dewey gave him an appraising look. She was fairly sure the boy was up to it, but didn't want to take any chances. They went to the little stable together, and Willy led Starbuck out into the sunshine. He looked at Midnight. Incarceration had left him glum.

"Willy, I need you to give me a very honest answer to a difficult question. Can you do that?"

"Sure, Mrs. James."

"Even though the answer may not be the one you want to give me."

"Yeah. Sure, I know. Like be candid."

"That's right. Like be candid."

"Okay."

"You told me that you rode Midnight over to the skeet range. And he didn't bolt."

"Nope. Not Midnight."

"Were there guns being fired?"

"Sure. The Marshy Point Ducking Club was having a skeet shoot. You know, like how they practice when it's not duck season."

"Yes. I am familiar with the ritual. It was perhaps not the

best place to go riding. But that's another matter. What did Midnight do?"

"He just kinda' reared a little. No problem. I know how to handle him, see."

"Yes. I really think you do."

"What's all this about, Mrs. James?"

Dewey gave herself one more minute to back out. But she couldn't. All she could do now was to hope that the morning would not end in cruel disaster.

"Willy, what would you say to a ride on Midnight this morning? Your honest answer. Can you handle him if he bolts?"

Willy was speechless for a moment. "Really?" he asked finally, in excited tones. "Really, Mrs. James?"

"Really, Willy."

Willy leaped in the air with joy and ran to tell the stallion the good news. "Midnight! Midnight! You're home free, old boy! We're going for a ride!"

Dewey was filled with misgiving.

Somehow, between the two of them, Willy and Dewey managed to get Starbuck's old saddle in working order. "He won't be comfortable, Willy, but it's the best I can do."

"He'll be okay, Mrs. James. Just look at him!"

Midnight Blue was the picture of a happy horse. He was munching contentedly on the grass in Dewey's back lawn, keeping the early-morning flies at bay with gentle swishing movements of his tail. His coal-black coat shone beautifully, giving back the morning sunlight. His ears were forward and his eyes were bright. Occasionally he stomped a foot; every now and then he let out a small snort.

"Yes, I think he'll do fine, Willy."

George Farnham arrived on the dot of seven-thirty.

"Morning, Willy."

"Heya!" said Willy cheerfully.

"I think you mean, good morning, Mr. Farnham," said Dewey.

"Right. Sorry, Mrs. James. Hi, Mr. Farnham. Midnight and I are going for a ride. Cool, huh?"

"Very cool," said George. He glowered at Dewey. "What's all this about, Dewey?"

"George, I think I'm in over my head."

She drew him aside, out of earshot of Willy. "I'd like you to phone Tack Marvin. Ask him to meet us at Barnhouse at eight-thirty. Will you do that?"

"Sure thing. Be right back." George headed indoors. Dewey and Willy finished cleaning up the stable and saddled Midnight. The boy was watching Dewey carefully as he tightened the girth.

"Uh, Mrs. James?"

"Yes, Willy."

"Is there something wrong?"

"I hope not."

"Can I just ride wherever I want on Midnight?"

"Yes, Willy; but I want you to meet me at Barnhouse in forty-five minutes. Between now and then, you can go wherever you like. But I want to see you there at eight-fifteen. Do you have a watch?"

"Yeah." Suddenly, Willy seemed to have lost his heart for this ride. He mounted and adjusted the stirrups. "Something's up, right?"

"Enjoy the ride, Willy." She gave Midnight a smack, and boy and stallion rode away.

George emerged from the kitchen. "He'll be there. Dewey, what on earth are you up to?"

"It's the end of an illustrious career, George." Dewey shook her head sadly. "Come and have coffee. Then would you mind driving us?"

"To Barnhouse?"

"To Barnhouse."

Leslie Downing was in the paddock when Dewey and George arrived. She looked competent and comfortable in jeans and a lightweight turtleneck; her short-cropped black hair swung freely in the sunlight as she stood in conversation with one of the grooms. If she was surprised by the arrival of her visitors, she was too polite to show it.

"Good morning, Leslie," said Dewey gravely.

"Hello, Dewey. Hello, George. Nice of you to come by. We can use a few friendly visitors these days."

"That was quite a speech you made to the town meeting the other night, Leslie," said George, somewhat at a loss. "I think the real-estate fiends have turned tail."

"I'm glad it was effective. They'll find some other property to rape, I'm sure."

"Undoubtedly," said George. "I admit that I was rather surprised that they hadn't looked into the water issue, however."

"You know how city folk are." Leslie Downing smiled. "They think everything just happens." They strolled over to sit on a bench outside the paddock. "What brings you here this morning?"

"Well," said Dewey sadly, "it's your horse, actually."

"Has something happened to him?"

"Oh, no. No, he's perfectly fine, Leslie. But I thought that it was time we resolved the situation. For everyone's sake, you know."

"You're absolutely right, Dewey. It was thoughtless of me to take advantage of your hospitality for so long. I'll send one of the boys over for him. And I suppose I'll have to send for Tack Marvin." She grew pale and looked away quickly.

"There's no need to send for Midnight. He's on his way."

"But—"

"And so is Doctor Marvin."

"I see. You seem to have thought of everything. That was kind of you."

"Midnight will be here shortly. But perhaps, before he gets here, you'd like to talk to us?"

"Oh, Dewey. When you have been through this kind of thing often enough, you get used to it. There is really nothing else to do, I'm afraid. It's painful, but I don't see a choice."

"No. I don't suppose you do." Dewey fell silent for a moment. "Because, of course, with Midnight out of the way, there won't be a witness, will there?"

Leslie Downing let out a short, baffled laugh. "What?"

"To the murder, Leslie."

"Ahh, Dewey, I don't think you quite—"

"Oh, I'm a crazy old lady, Leslie. But you know, I happen to be right about this."

Suddenly there came the sound of thundering hooves, and Willy emerged from beyond a turn in the driveway, taking Midnight up the dirt road in a beautiful canter. When he got within two hundred yards, he slowed to a walk and headed straight for the paddock, where Dewey and George were talking to Leslie Downing.

"Hey, Mrs. Downing!" Willy called cheerfully. "Look who's back in action!" He brought the horse straight toward them.

Leslie Downing looked up, her beautiful face a frozen mask.

"Careful, Willy," called Dewey. "Careful."

"He did great, Mrs. James!" Boy and horse were now within a half a dozen yards of the little group.

Suddenly, Midnight flattened his ears and gave voice to a piercing whinny, an agonized cry fraught with unmistakable terror. Dewey and George watched in horror as Midnight's eyes rolled crazily in their sockets, and he reared back violently.

Willy was unprepared, but not daunted. He concentrated on the horse. "Steady, Midnight, steady!" he called, as he hung on fiercely. He gave a strong tug at the reins and succeeded in turning the horse. The stable hands began to gather to watch the contest between the redheaded boy and the coal-black stallion. Willy hung on for all he was worth as the horse reared again and again. Finally, finding himself unable to shake his rider, Midnight bolted. The little crowd stared in amazement as Midnight took the fence into the south enclosure. Then he galloped madly away across the field, like one who'd come face to face with the devil.

33

"THAT WAS A dangerous stunt you pulled, Dewey," said Fielding Booker. "The boy might have been killed."

Shortly after Willy's rapid disappearance across the south enclosure, Dewey had summoned Booker. The policeman had met with a curiously grim scene on his arrival. After a word of hurried consultation with George and Dewey, he had charged Leslie Downing with the murder of Donald Irish.

"Don't be silly, Bookie. I knew he would be fine. It was Midnight I was concerned about."

"Dewey, really," said Booker.

"Really, Bookie. My worry was that Willy would somehow get to Barnhouse before us, and that Leslie would put Midnight down before we had a chance to stop her."

They were sitting once more in George Farnham's kitchen. It was the end of another very long day, and everyone was tired. George had cooked them supper, and had graciously included both Willy and Booker in the feast.

Over the fried chicken, Willy had related to them every minute of his hair-raising ride. After supper, Jack Grimes had called to pick his son up; Willy had departed energetically, leaving the three exhausted adults to drink coffee and talk over the case.

"Besides, Bookie," Dewey pointed out, "if I had told you what I wanted to do, you would have thought I was crazy."

"I don't know why you say that. I fell for all the other clues you fed me." He shook his head.

"No, Bookie," interjected George. "You would never have

196

believed that a horse could testify so eloquently. You'll have to admit it." He looked at Dewey. "I wouldn't have, either. Dewey tricked me into going with her. But I wish you had seen it. It was really something. Made the hair on the back of my neck stand up."

"Dewey was slow in sending out my invitation to her party," said Booker. "I had to wait for the second seating."

When Booker had arrived at the scene, Leslie Downing, with a directness that was typical of her, had confessed at once. "I'd rather get it all over with, if you please, Captain," she had said to Booker. "Mrs. James seems to have ferreted out my little secret. And I'd rather not waste any more energy on this charade." Then she made her statement.

It was simple and to the point. She had discovered on Irish's desk at Barnhouse a document that had, for some reason, piqued her curiosity. She read it, never dreaming at first that it had anything to do with her. It was a letter addressed to Irish; in it was a mention of proposed condominiums on Smallpoint Hill. That was the little hill directly behind Leslie Downing's house.

Before confronting Irish, she had gone to the state capital and done some digging—exactly the same kind of research that Dewey and George had done in town. She found that, in exchange for a loan, Irish had used his power of attorney to grant a security interest in her horses to a corporation she had never heard of.

"The famous Questor, Inc.," said Dewey, as Booker told his story. "I thought that name sounded phony."

"It was just a shell corporation," said Booker. "The lenders were really the Aviance partners. Irish worked for them."

"He probably stood to make a fortune by turning over the property to them," speculated Dewey. "What did you find out about Irish's scheme today, Bookie?"

"Oh, it was ingenious. His plan was to drain away all the cash, leaving the business exposed. Then he probably would have offered her a choice—the horses, or the property." He paused. "By the way, Dewey, how did you get an idea about all of this?"

"It seemed clear there was something strange going on.

Those developers were prepared to spend a fortune—for property without water rights! I reasoned that perhaps they had been sure of the water rights, somehow. Which meant Barnhouse. But if Barnhouse was flourishing, Leslie would never budge. I just turned the picture upside-down, and assumed that the financial health of Barnhouse was a mirage. If you worked from there, it was clear."

"Abracadabra, as Hugh said to me," added Booker.

"How did you find out about the UCC filings, Dewey?" asked George.

"The notebook that Hugh found."

"Ah, yes," interposed Booker. "Leslie said that she had a lawyer looking into things down at the state capital. They were notes he had taken, I gather."

"How did you know what the notes meant, Dewey?" pursued George.

"I asked an expert to decipher them for me," she answered vaguely.

George grumbled. "Your felonious beau," he said unhappily. "You could have asked me, Dewey."

"George, you have very little experience of crooked business practices. We hope. Don't take it so hard." She smiled at him.

"I may know a lot more in a month or two. This leaves Barnhouse in rather a curious position, legally. I expect the Aviance vultures will return, to pick over the leavings. Peter has asked me to represent his mother's interests."

"That's thoughtful of Peter," said Dewey.

"I think it's really for Hugh's sake. He can manage the place, until then. If he decides not to leave town."

"Then Peter wasn't involved in the real estate deal at all, Bookie?" questioned Dewey.

"No," said Booker. "It was another lawyer from his firm. That was just a lucky coincidence. Or unlucky. But Leslie didn't know that. She was going to cut Peter out of her will."

"Instead, she got sidetracked into murder," said George.

"Yes," said Dewey. "It must have been quite plausible to invite Irish for a walk on Friday night. It was a chilly evening; I imagine she put her gloves on. All very natural."

"That's what she said in her statement," agreed Booker.

Dewey continued. "It must have been a simple thing to lead him down through that little grove of trees near the house, where the fence timbers were. She could just reach down, pick one up, and whack him over the head."

"What a cool customer," said George. There was more than a hint of admiration in his tone. "Did she tell you how she got him into the stable, Bookie? She can't be that strong."

"She's pretty strong. But she went and got the blanket out of Willy's shed, and dragged Irish on top of it. He wasn't quite dead yet, so she had to finish him off. Then, later, she dragged him down the hill to the stable. A matter of five minutes."

"While Peter and Hugh were out on their strolls?" asked George. "That seems a little risky, even for someone like Leslie Downing."

"Oh, she must have waited. Did she wait, Bookie?"

Booker nodded, taking a sip of coffee. "She says she went to bed, then got up again at three. Moved the body into Midnight's stall."

"That was a nasty trick to play on Midnight," George pointed out.

"I imagine she thought nothing would faze him," said Dewey. "He's a remarkable horse."

"What was Hugh doing on his mysterious errand?" George refilled everyone's coffee cup.

"Thanks, George," said Booker. "I think he went to talk to Leslie. He was puzzled about that notebook, you remember."

"Yes," said Dewey. "And found she wasn't at home. Poor Hugh. He was loyal to her to the last. He never said a word about her being out that night, did he, Bookie?"

"Nope. Silly old coot."

"I think he's in love with her," said George. "I think he's always been in love with her."

They sat in silence for a few moments.

"I suppose that Gordon fellow tied into it, somehow," said George.

"Yes, he must have," put in Dewey. "As I see it, the plan must have been to fix a few races so Leslie would lose her standing."

"Yes," agreed Booker. "It must have been something like that. Sergeant Fenton says the racing association watches the owners pretty carefully. You can be banned from racing if they catch you at anything."

"That would have ruined her absolutely," said Dewey.

"That man Irish was a swine," said George.

"How did Hugh take it, Bookie?"

"Just as you might expect. He didn't say much, but I think he was dreadfully hurt. I've seen a lot of that kind of thing, one way and another, in this business. Does a lot of damage."

"She's an ice queen, that Leslie Downing."

"A veritable Lady Macbeth. She had no compunctious visitings of nature, at any rate," said Dewey thoughtfully. "Hugh Shields was probably the best friend she ever had. And like a father to Peter—that's why Peter argued with Irish. He was trying to stand up for Hugh." They brooded in silence. "I don't see how Leslie Downing could have betrayed him so cruelly."

"Tony Zimmerman would have gotten Hugh off," said George. "Bookie, you'll have to admit your case was circumstantial at best." He thought for a minute. "Too bad about all that hard evidence—those fence posts and blankets and so forth. You were so sure about them."

"Oh, I'm still sure about them. They were used to do the murder, just as we thought all along."

"How did Hugh get hold of the blanket, then?" asked George.

"I imagine he found it in the tack shed," said Dewey. "All cleaned up and ready to go. He took it for Willy. Then he had to lie to Bookie about it. Right, Bookie?" Booker nodded as Dewey continued. "He's crazy about that boy. And if the police got hold of it, there would be no telling how many years it might take them to give it up again."

"We do need the evidence in a capital murder case, Dewey," protested Booker.

"Of course you do," said Dewey placatingly. "It's just as well. Because the horse didn't race, did he? So the blanket is moot."

"What I can't get over," said George, "is that she killed the man she was going to marry."

"Oh, she wasn't going to marry that clown, George." Dewey sounded shocked at the very idea.

"She wasn't?" asked Booker.

"Of course not. Can you imagine it?"

"But everybody said so," George protested. "Didn't they, Bookie?"

Booker considered. "No. Remarkable, isn't it? In fact, nobody said so, George. Except for Leslie Downing." He smiled at his sudden enlightenment, recalling how she had told him of their engagement. "She was so dignified when she told me. So gracious in her hour of loss. I was really impressed. I thought it was true love."

"The only thing she ever loved is those horses," said Dewey sadly. "That's the kind of love that leads to murder."

George roused himself from the contemplation of Leslie Downing's dignified grief. "How on earth did you know, Dewey?"

"Simple, really." She smiled at both men. "She never came to see Midnight."

"Oh, come on, Dewey, you are carrying this horse thing a bit too far." Booker sounded really indignant.

"I promise you, Bookie. If you think about it, you'll see what I mean."

"And you worked out why she never came?" George asked.

"Eventually. Midnight is very valuable. For that reason alone I would have expected her to call. Leslie also loves him madly. I assumed that she couldn't bear to put him down; that she was ignoring the issue in the hope that it would go away."

"But?" asked Booker.

"But then, you know, we found it was a case of murder. No question that the horse had had anything to do with it. Except for being on the spot. A witness—or so it appeared to me. There was no compelling reason to put him down; yet I got a sense, when I talked to Hugh, that she still intended to do it."

"I see," said George.

"Yes. And the only reason for that, that I could think of, was that Midnight presented a threat, somehow. Luckily, she hesitated. She probably couldn't bring herself to do it. And that left me time to puzzle over it."

"Dewey, you really are remarkably clever," said Booker.

"Oh, I don't think cleverness had anything to do with it, Bookie. It was just an idea that turned into an obsession. You might say it was my *bête noir*."

Dewey was saddened, if not altogether surprised, by how quickly the whole episode of the murder faded from the collective consciousness of her good neighbors. By midsummer's night, the life of poor Donald Irish was no more than an indifferent footnote to the interesting events at Barnhouse. He was absorbed into Hamilton history—or at least into its stock of anecdotes—there to be forgotten, except when his brief moment in the sun was recalled.

The trial was short and to the point. Both judge and defendant disliked unnecessary activity, preferring to be straightforward in their dealings. A guilty plea was entered and a sentence was handed down; it was all rather matter-of-fact, if you considered the enormity of the crime. Many people in town were disappointed by the absence of spectacular effects from the proceedings.

But perhaps that was just as well. There were many other things to get on with, now that summer was here. Hamiltonians diverted their attention to newly compelling issues. And, across the remarkably beautiful countryside, a brave, red-headed boy spent his mornings flying like the wind astride a gentle coal-black stallion.